DEAD ENTRY

BBC BOOKS

This book is based on the BBC TV
series *Dead Entry* by Allan Baker,
produced by Paul Stone and directed
by Margie Barbour. The main
characters were played as follows:
Charlie, Duncan Baizley; Melissa,
Lise-Ann McLaughlin; Daniel, Rhett
Keen; Richard Avery, Geoffrey
Bateman.

Published by BBC Books,
a division of BBC Enterprises Ltd,
35 Marylebone High Street, London W1M 4AA

First published 1987
© Allan Baker 1987
ISBN 0 563 20566 0

Photoset by Rowland Phototypesetting Ltd,
Bury St Edmunds, Suffolk

Printed in England by Butler & Tanner Ltd,
Frome and London

Acknowledgements

By putting a computer within my financial range Amstrad made me think seriously about computing. These thoughts in turn led to the story that is told in these pages. The script and later the novel were both written on a word processor, and for kindly placing this at my disposal, I wish to express my sincere thanks to Amstrad.

Paul Stone and Margie Barbour, who, respectively, produced and directed *Dead Entry*, have given plentifully and productively. For their ideas, suggestions, advice and above all good humour I am most grateful.

The briefest acknowledgement conceals the greatest debt. My thanks to Richard Krupp.

For Jorge Santos,
who showed me that tenacity,
curiosity and candour
are the essence of childhood
and creation.

ONE

It had been Charlie's idea to make the trip to the docks at Avonmouth. Under normal circumstances the docks wouldn't even have made the short list of half-term excursions. Even if you were interested in ships – and neither Charlie nor his friend Daniel were – you could see all the ships you wanted in the centre of Bristol. For one thing, there was far more variety down at the city centre basin, with sailboats and speedboats and yachts and dinghies and even a floating museum. The only things you could count on seeing at Avonmouth were cargo ships, and, after all, a consignment of emeralds looked no more exciting than one of tractor wheels: everything arrived in containers and they all looked exactly the same.

The two boys hadn't come to the docks looking for excitement. On the contrary, they had set out with the very highest of motives. This was an educational excursion on a par with a school trip to the Science Museum in London or to Warwick Castle. What's more, this one was voluntary. They were undertaking it without any coercion. It was an added bonus that there wouldn't be an essay to write or questions to answer afterwards.

It was in Mr Mellors' class, Environmental Geography, that Charlie and Daniel had first heard mention of the *Sea Shepherd*. Later, there had been a short item on the regional TV news and a picture of the ship being re-fitted down in the Avonmouth docks. The ship used to be a fishing boat catching herring up on the north coast of Scotland. A local Bristol businessman had recently bought her and was converting her into a pollution patrol ship.

Just a few weeks ago Charlie and Daniel spent a Saturday with Mr Mellors. Their teacher and a group of his friends sacrificed one day a month to help restore a disused canal. There were people repointing the brickwork while others scythed the weeds that overran the banks.

The two boys had lent a hand and were amazed to see such things as a rusty bedstead and an old gas cooker hauled up from the canal bed. Until then, they had never really been aware that humans were the main cause of environmental pollution. It was this revelation that prompted them to go and look at the *Sea Shepherd* for themselves.

*   *   *   *   *

Daniel was sitting on an upended wooden crate in the back of a tarpaulin-covered lorry. It was dark inside with the flap now lowered all the way down. With his right hand he held on to one of the wooden struts that ran along the side of the lorry. He made to shift his foot and was suddenly aware of a tacky substance, like chewing gum, holding onto the crepe sole of his running shoes. He hoped it was only chewing gum, and made a face.

'This is another fine mess you've got me into,

Stanley.' In the darkness Daniel looked across to where he imagined Charlie to be.

'It's no use blaming me,' Charlie answered with some defiance. He knew it wasn't his fault. He couldn't have guessed that there would be a security man at the entrance to the dock. In fact, he felt rather proud at having the daring to suggest they get into the docks by hiding themselves inside a lorry. He was holding onto the grille behind the driver's cabin and could hear the driver greeting the security man. This was followed by the sound of the gate lifting in front of them.

'We've just gone past the gate,' Charlie whispered. 'We'll jump out when he stops, right?'

'I need to have a pee,' Daniel complained.

The driver accelerated suddenly, throwing Charlie against the side of the lorry. They travelled on for another minute or two and lurched forwards as the driver braked sharply. The lorry stopped shuddering and the cab door slammed shut.

'Okay, let's go.' The boys peered cautiously out from under the tarpaulin, then quickly jumped out and raced for cover.

Dirty grey water swirled and slapped against the concrete walls of the jetty. Giant, rusting cranes like prehistoric stick insects stood rigidly along the jutting piers. Pulleys swayed in the wind from thick chains. Just a few ships were scattered here and there, and soot-covered warehouses stretched along the wharf-side, their windows bricked up. Sheets of loose corrugated roofing beat against the exposed eaves in the wind. There wasn't a sign of life anywhere. The docks were depressing, a wasteland. The machinery reminded Charlie of the stripped skeletons of fairground

9

pleasure rides before the coloured lights and gaudily painted fronts had been fastened on.

Charlie shivered and dug his hands into the pockets of his anorak, suddenly gloomy. He swivelled his head from side to side scanning the horizon, looking for the *Sea Shepherd*. Daniel briskly scraped the sole of his trainer against a cobblestone.

'This place is huge.' Charlie sighed. 'It'll take ages to find the *Sea Shepherd*.'

'Don't be daft, Charlie,' Daniel chided. He was impatient, sensing that Charlie's enthusiasm was waning. Now that they were no longer safely concealed in the rear of the lorry, Charlie began to feel afraid. Daniel looked around, his eyes darting left and right. He knew it was important to stay out of sight and reconnoitre the dock from a protected position, to discover as much about the geography of the place as possible with the least risk of detection. He spied a parking bay with several towers of stacked wooden pallets. It would be an ideal hiding place. They could climb up the sides and get a better view.

'Look, there's some wooden crates over there. It can be our base camp.'

They ran down the cobbled road at full speed. There were railway tracks buried in the road but from the rust it was obvious there hadn't been a train running through here in many years. Daniel slipped in between two stacks of pallets. Charlie followed behind. The pallets rose about a metre above their heads. There was no chance of being seen here. Charlie picked up a discarded crate and set it on its end. He climbed on top and looked over the battlements. They were at a crossroads where four piers joined the main inner dock road. It was a perfect lookout. Daniel took one of the little alleyways and performed his urgent act of nature.

'What's the matter, DL? . . . Lost your bottle?' Charlie felt his confidence return now that they were out of danger's way. Suddenly, there was a loud noise. It startled Charlie. He climbed back onto his crate and cautiously raised his head. The noise, a crisp, snapping sound, had come from one of the small cranes. It was the sound of the metal teeth sinking into the grooves of the gears.

'What on earth was that?'

Charlie watched as a winch began slowly hauling up a thick, oil-stained rope. 'They're pulling something out of the sea.'

'Get down and let's have a look, then,' said Daniel, coming back towards Charlie. 'What is it?'

'I don't know yet.' Charlie suddenly gasped in surprise. 'There's an ambulance over there, too.'

'Let's see, then,' Daniel pleaded. 'Give us a chance.'

'Looks like someone's had an accident.'

Daniel was growing irritated with the constant commentary and Charlie's selfishness with the crate.

'Move over, give us some room.' Daniel climbed up beside Charlie and balanced with one foot on the crate and another wedged between the pallets. They watched as the winch chugged steadily. A few seconds later a net leapt out of the sea. As the water drained away Charlie saw what looked like a giant wellington boot inside the net. He turned to Daniel to make a joke about it. But Daniel had already turned to him.

'It's a body, Charlie. Someone's drowned.'

Charlie shivered. He felt a ribbon of sweat across his forehead. Daniel swallowed hard, felt his stomach

11

somersault. 'I don't want to see any more. Really, I don't . . .' Daniel whispered. There were splinters of agony in his voice.

Charlie tried to unfasten his gaze from the scene. But he continued to stare. A desperate curiosity took hold of him. He saw now that the body was a man in a wetsuit, a diver. He had an obstinate urge to witness the proof that inside the wetsuit there was a human body. He felt hypnotised. It was like watching an egg and waiting for a chick to hatch and peck its way through the shell.

The net hovered over the ground. A man stretched out his arm and grabbed at it. The net swung wildly, and the diver's neck rolled limply from side to side. Charlie felt his stomach pitching. The man finally managed to secure the net with both hands and lowered it to the ground. As he turned the net around, water spilled from the diver's boots.

The back door of the ambulance opened and another man walked across to where the body lay. He was holding something in the crook of his elbow. He took it with his other hand and flicked it with his wrist. A black plastic sheet unfurled and fluttered to the ground. Meanwhile, the man with wispy silver hair squatted on his haunches. He lifted the diver's hand and squeezed the diver's wrist to verify what the ambulanceman had already anticipated. The diver was now officially and authoritatively dead.

Daniel scrambled back up and stood beside Charlie. He was just in time to see the old man – a doctor, probably – peel off the diver's rubber face-mask. '*That* is what I call gruesome.'

Charlie watched as the ambulanceman bent down

and spread out the plastic sheet. Now the doctor came around and helped fold the edges together. They were quite as meticulous as Charlie's mother when she collected the bedclothes from the garden drying line.

'They're putting him in the back of the ambulance now.' Charlie had resumed his commentary. Somehow, the act of reporting what was happening to Daniel made Charlie less involved and at the same time provided him with an excuse to carry on looking.

Daniel hunched his shoulders and sucked his teeth. None of this was his concern. 'Can we go now, please . . . or do you want to stay and see a shipwreck maybe, or even a plane crash?'

'I don't know what you're talking about,' Charlie answered sharply. 'I only came here to see the *Sea Shepherd*, that's all.' Charlie's face reddened, flushed with anger, as if he was being accused of having planned the accident in the first place. What Daniel said was ridiculous, ludicrous.

'I'm ready when you are. Forget the diver. Forget we ever saw anything.'

*   *   *   *   *

A sudden breeze tousled Martin Galbraith's hair. The salty air stung his eyes. It was a chilly October morning and his freshly shaved cheeks smarted. He stood with his hands deep in his trouser pockets and looked around. The only good thing to be said for the day so far was that there had been one stroke of luck. At least we're quite isolated out here, he thought to himself. Away from prying eyes.

Tony Hughes got out of the car and slapped the door shut. Hughes had entered the police force from university and had only spent three months as a detective constable before his sergeant excused him from duty one morning and handed him a short letter. He was to attend an interview at New Scotland Yard. There and then he was offered a transfer to Special Branch. He had been seconded to another department under Galbraith's leadership four months ago. But Galbraith wasn't police; he was army, or used to be. Nobody used rank titles. Hughes didn't know whether they existed in MI5.

Galbraith watched as Hughes made his way towards him. He observed that Hughes was wearing a double-breasted grey cashmere overcoat with the collar raised at the neck.

'Murphy's law, I guess,' Hughes commented.

'Oh, yes,' answered Galbraith vaguely. 'And what would that be?' He was finding Hughes more of an irritation with every hour.

Hughes reddened a little as he realised his blunder. Never make your superior officer feel less intelligent than you, he reminded himself. Don't do or say anything to get up their nose. Keep an amicable distance, don't get too friendly. He looked at Galbraith and was unable to stop himself from thinking that Galbraith was, indeed, his inferior.

'Murphy's law . . .' He paused, wondering how to give an explanation that wouldn't expose Galbraith's ignorance. 'It's just something we used to say at school. A sort of joke, I suppose, like Einstein's laws of the theory of relativity. Murphy's law just says that anything that can go wrong always will.'

'That's what I call sod's law.' Galbraith snorted and watched the policemen roll the diver's body in the black plastic shroud. He spoke again, this time

14

exaggerating his Northern Irish accent. 'We don't go in for many Irish jokes where I come from. If you don't like a knee-capping. What's the news?'

'Mr Nicholson is taking the lunchtime train.'

Galbraith didn't reply. Nicholson was one of the half-dozen Deputies who reigned over the nation's internal security. He was Head of 'D' Branch, the section which monitored the Soviets and their satellite activities on home ground. Galbraith gloomily pondered the dead diver before him. The tide was turning against him. Months of careful, scrupulously careful, observation and surveillance had already passed. An impressive machine had been set in place. It had functioned with easy efficiency. He had started the whole thing from scratch and hadn't gone a penny over budget. Even with the odd claim for overtime from the watchers he was still well within his contingency budget. Now, the whole thing was collapsing before his eyes. He had sent a man to his death. And, to add insult to injury, the diver wasn't even one of his outfit. He'd lost a Navy man. He just prayed that Nicholson had been in the Air Force or the Army.

The doctor walked over to Galbraith. 'I shan't be writing a report, of course, Mr Galbraith. Perhaps I can telephone you with my findings?' he suggested.

'Perhaps you'd like to tell me them now, doctor,' Galbraith ventured. 'And save yourself the 10p.'

The doctor lowered his eyelids. He understood that Galbraith's facetiousness was no more than a symptom of anxiety. 'I shall have to do a further examination, of course. A post mortem. But I don't have a great deal to tell you until after that.'

'I've got a pathologist lined up already, thanks all the same.'

Doctor Sands looked pained.

Galbraith had needlessly humiliated him. He regretted it now but it was too late.

'I can't understand why you called me then. You obviously don't need me here.'

'He mightn't have been dead. You might have been able to save him,' said Galbraith, trying to compensate for his tactlessness. He could see, though, that Sands wasn't so easily mollified.

'I'm only a country doctor, Mr Galbraith. I can't work miracles.' Sands drew his stomach in and thrust his chest out. 'But I have no doubt *you* can.' He smiled lightly, knowing the catastrophe was all Galbraith's.

Doctor Sands walked away to his car. Galbraith saw Hughes chatting with the driver of the ambulance. The driver had lit a cigarette. They were all loaded up and ready to go. The cold sea air sliced through his unlined cotton jacket and Galbraith recalled the isolation and bitter cold of his many winters in Carrickfergus. He hated the sea. Death revolted him. He stamped his feet to bring the blood back into his legs.

Hughes called across. 'All done, sir?'

They walked back to their unmarked car together. Neither of them spoke. The tall, unwieldy cranes around the several piers were strangely ominous. Scavengers, vultures, thought Galbraith. It was a bleak day. Things were going to get worse before they got better.

Hughes opened the door for Galbraith. He never forgot the little courtesies due a ranking officer. Galbraith yanked the seat belt across his body and

16

fastened it home. Hughes got into the driver's seat and started the engine.

'Shall we radio HQ before we leave, sir?'

Galbraith picked up the handset of the car radio and then replaced it. Regulations stated he should check in with base HQ before leaving the scene of an incident. Bad news can wait, thought Galbraith. He signalled to Hughes to drive off.

'I'll tell them it was out of order,' he said. 'A touch of Murphy's law with the old walkie-talkie.' Hughes carefully aimed the car down the bumpy cobblestone road.

The ambulance with the dead body wrapped in the black plastic sheet followed an even distance behind. Once they were off the rippled road and safely once more on blacktop, Hughes quickly shifted into fourth gear. The ambulance meandered at a more leisurely pace. Hughes took a corner in third, a little ostentatiously it seemed to Galbraith, demonstrating the skills he'd acquired on his advanced driving course at the police college in Hendon.

'Watch out, laddie!' Galbraith yelled suddenly.

Two lads of about fifteen years had just materialised from nowhere. They were jaywalking where they had no right to be. One of them was deaf to the noise of the car, insulated from the world with a Walkman on his ears.

Hughes thumped the horn. The second boy grabbed his friend's arm and threw him against the side of an old warehouse.

'I've a mind to stop the car and nick the pair of them,' Hughes screeched angrily. 'They've no right to be here in the first place.'

17

A TV detector van zipped out from the cover of a warehouse and joined the convoy.

'No one said what his name was.' Galbraith's thoughts were elsewhere.

'Sands, sir. Doctor Sands. Ex-infantry regiment,' prompted Hughes helpfully.

'Not the quack,' growled Galbraith. 'I meant the poor damn diver lad. I don't even know his name. And I have to tell his family.'

TWO

Charlie stared after the car as it drove away towards the road that led out of the docks. The sudden pounding on the car horn had frightened him. It had scared him more than the sight of the lifeless diver. Or, perhaps, his reaction now was a kind of delayed shock. His heart was in his mouth, pumping away behind his cheek. He could feel the side of his mouth swelling and shrinking. He wondered now what he would say to his mother about what he and Daniel had seen. He could already hear her voice and her disapproving tone. 'In the first place . . .' she was saying '. . . you had absolutely no right to be in the docks. And, in the second . . .' Charlie made a resolution to keep his mouth shut and not to mention the visit at all.

Daniel was walking on tiptoe along the sunken railway tracks in the quayside road, swaying, his arms stuck out like a trapeze artist on a high wire. Charlie joined in with the game. Daniel smiled. Subject closed, he was hoping.

'Dan, I'll make you a bet,' Charlie said brightly.

'I think I'll pass, if it's all the same to you,' replied Daniel, cautiously. Somehow, Charlie's bets were never to his advantage. Daniel always stood to lose something he prized while Charlie only had on offer something Daniel never much wanted anyway. 'Not today, okay? Besides, look over there . . .' he pointed excitedly. 'It's the *Sea Shepherd*, Charlie. We've found her at last!'

The ship was being repainted all in white. Along the side there were huge paintings of animals – tortoises, giraffes, eagles – with a looping rainbow threading between them. She was small in size compared to the cargo ships in the docks, just over 200 tons. In her new livery, though, she would have been difficult to miss: she stood out like a punk rocker at a coronation.

The boys stood on the quayside. Daniel tilted his head and looked up, his hand over his eyes. 'Doesn't look like anyone's on board,' he said to Charlie. A gangway led up to the deck. 'You game?'

Charlie hesitated. He was beginning to regret ever having suggested visiting the *Sea Shepherd*. The day was threatening to produce nothing but a chain of misdemeanours and misfortunes. First, they smuggle themselves into the docks in the back of a lorry. Second, they accidentally witness a dead body being recovered from the sea. And now they're just about to wander onto a boat uninvited and probably get arrested for trespassing. Charlie wished earnestly that ships had front doors you could knock on or a bell to ring. Daniel was already half way up the gangway. He whistled to Charlie between his teeth. Well, if someone's on board, thought Charlie, they know now they've got company. He started to climb the sloping ladder.

Daniel's whistle had just this effect. A young man with golden hair now appeared at the top of the steps beside the bridge. Charlie stopped in his tracks. 'Hello!'

the man shouted. 'What can I do for you?' Charlie was tongue-tied.

'Wotcha!' Daniel shouted back in reply. 'We're ecologists – trainees. We came miles to have a quick look round the boat. Is it okay?'

'Come on up,' came the generous and unexpected reply. Daniel turned to Charlie with an expression of undisguised triumph. Charlie mounted the ramp and joined Daniel on the slatted wood deck. It was strewn with packing cases, tea chests, oil drums and just plain old litter. The man descended from the bridge and stretched out his hand.

'Hi. I'm called Lasse.'

'After the dog?' asked Daniel, puzzled. Charlie could see their visit becoming very short indeed if things carried on like this.

'I doubt it,' Lasse replied with a friendly smile. 'It's a Swedish name, quite common, but not for animals I don't think.'

'I'm Daniel. And this is Charlie.' Daniel stretched out his hand to shake Lasse's, pleased with the adult formality.

'We learned all about the *Sea Shepherd* from our geography teacher at school,' explained Charlie. 'We've been learning all about pollution and ecology and food chains and things, and next term we have to pick one aspect for a project and Daniel and I thought we'd do toxic waste, so we wanted to come and see the ship first,' Charlie paused finally and drew his breath, then continued, 'in case it seemed too hard.'

Lasse smiled at Charlie's nervous loquacity. 'Well, you've certainly come to the right place.'

Lasse led them first to the bridge which he said

would be the hub of operations once the ship was on the high seas. He opened the door of the wheelhouse. The traditional wheel was there but otherwise the instruments reminded the boys more of Cape Kennedy than the Cutty Sark. There were rows of computer video screens, revolving barrels with graph paper being traced by a marker, keyboards of all descriptions. Charlie experienced the thrill of familiarity, and Daniel immediately noticed the change that had come over his friend. His diffidence, his shyness dissipated. He no longer felt awkward or an intruder.

'He's got microchips in the blood,' declared Daniel by way of explanation. He felt proud of Charlie's expert ability with computers but knew that his friend would not mention this himself.

Lasse turned and addressed Charlie directly. 'Then you have started off on the right foot. It is not enough simply to be concerned any more. What we must do is very technical, highly complicated. We must care, of course . . . but also, we must be trained scientists to devise and comprehend the experiments we must undertake.' Charlie at once nodded vigorously in agreement. He indicated Daniel. '*He* has trouble using a calculator!'

'Well, Columbus didn't even have a slide rule and he still managed to discover America,' Daniel retorted, defensively.

Lasse intervened quickly to diffuse any disagreement. 'You're right, Daniel. Absolutely. It is more important to have passion and a curiosity about the world. Otherwise all one's knowledge is pointless. There must be a dream. You must have the belief that it is possible to make your own mark on the world.

22

Without that, learning is sterile. We must use our education to improve both our lives and the life of the world we live in.'

A silence followed Lasse's impassioned speech. For a moment he wasn't sure if his evangelistic fervour hadn't had the opposite effect to that which he'd intended. He wondered whether the two boys were enthused or deterred. His own intense commitment, he knew from experience, often made people feel over-awed.

Daniel chewed his lip. Charlie's admiring eyes swept over the banked rows of computers and screens. He tried to guess how many hundreds of thousands of pounds' worth of hardware filled the room. He wondered at the cost of the whole enterprise. Then he remembered what Mr Mellors, the geography teacher, had said a private benefactor, a computer millionaire, had generously offered to equip the ship and finance the three-month voyage. Charlie cast around in his memory for the man's name. It almost flew at him.

'Is Mr Avery here? I'd really like to meet him. It's fantastic what he's done.'

Lasse shook his head. 'You just missed him, as a matter of fact. He only left about ten minutes ago. We were running a test programme on one of the new computers.'

Daniel glanced at the mass of hardware. 'What exactly are you going to do with all this machinery? I thought you'd have test tubes and bunsen burners and things like that.'

A grin unfurled acros Lasse's face. The aim of the operation seemed simple to the boys. The *Sea Shepherd* was supposed to be clearing up the polluted seas. They expected to find huge stores of ammonia, Dettol and bleach, not useless computers.

'Here, you see,' he explained, fingering a few keys on a keyboard, 'we have the complete records of all the prevous toxic waste surveys that have been taken in our target region.' Rows and columns of figures rained across the green screen. 'Readings are taken at precise intervals based on latitudes and longitudes. Now we shall go to the same place, the exact spot, and repeat the experiments to compare analyses.'

'Like the man who comes to read the electric meter?'

Lasse nodded. 'Exactly.'

*   *   *   *   *

Melissa – again – chose the scenic route to work. Hope springs eternal, she reminded herself. The newspaper offices were in the centre of Bristol trussed by the impenetrable one-way system. There was always a traffic jam and Melissa could blame her late arrival on the 'motoring conditions'. She dipped her indicator and swung out in an arc to join the outer ring road. The detour took her part of the way along the periphery road parallel to the River Avon. And under the suspension bridge.

Melissa Nelson liked to think of herself as unfettered: she hated having restraints imposed on her. She was a determined and accomplished reporter, only just over 26, who had won her spurs in a battle with the city council that had resulted in their cancelling a redevelopment scheme. She took no nonsense, spoke her mind. Proudly single, she was her own woman. Today she had streaked her blonde hair green.

Melissa's hope was likely to be someone else's misfortune. The only newsworthy bridge story these days was a good old-fashioned suicide. Of course, there were always students parachuting on elastic bands, abseilers, hang-gliders and a variety of novelty publicity seekers. All of them were to be ignored. They were cranks and show-offs. Melissa felt no interest either in students trying to finance a new full-size billiard table or a bed in a hostel for ex-offenders. This sort of story was her bread and butter. It made her choke with resentment. She was suffocating on it.

She looked up to the summit of Clifton. A few runners were exhausting themselves pointlessly trying to ascend the winding path that led to the peak. Melissa knew enough about exercise to know that the important thing was to maintain pace and so rhythm and breath control. It seemed to her that either these runners were martyring themselves for the sake of a good view or, more likely, frauds who when they got to the top would skip across to the newsagents for a *Guardian* and twenty Silk Cut. She noticed a TV detector van parked on the promenade. A good place to have a coffee break and study the form for the evening dogs.

Melissa calculated the odds on her future with the *Bristol Evening Echo*. It was a thousand times better here than it would be at the *Angling Times* or *The Grocer*. She knew that the editor Bernard Dougherty was indulgent towards her; perhaps he felt a sort of fatherly protectiveness, or perhaps he secretly sympathised with her determined ambition and the calculating manner she would need if she were to move on to one of the national dailies. She knew Dougherty would expect her to be honest and consistent in her reply to his charges. He would respect her for her principles. She made her defence an attack.

25

'Give me a half-way decent assignment, Bernie,' she proclaimed when she arrived twenty minutes late, 'and I'll write you a damn good piece. I've had enough of feeding off the scraps. All I get is the offal. Weddings, meals-on-wheels ladies, the Guides. You'd go crazy, too, if all you were offered was this bland nonsense. You know I'm a good journalist. Stop punishing me.'

Dougherty was calm, still. His bulk seemed to absorb Melissa's angry outburst. He now appeared to be digesting it. He placed his hand over his stomach and belched. 'Don't give my ulcer a tantrum, Melissa, please,' he pleaded. 'I've put a little something special aside, just for you. This is real champagne and truffles.'

Melissa plucked at the underside of her knee where her tights scrubbed against the sensitive skin. She trusted blindly to the messages her anatomy emitted. It was her own very refined and quite individual Tarot. Something interesting was in the ether.

'I'm on tenterhooks, Bernie. Tell me, please,' she said. 'It's not the Royals, is it?'

Dougherty laughed for the first time that morning. One minute he'd imagined Melissa as a budding James Cameron and the next she reveals herself a precocious Lady Olga Maitland. 'Not the Royals, I'm afraid. Not even a title in sight. At least, not yet.' He blurted it out. 'But if you strut your stuff in the usual inimitable style . . . who knows? I want you to do me a profile, maybe even more than one, on Richard Avery. In a month or so he's launching this ecological ship he's financed, sending it off to measure how much crap and arsenic and old lace we're all dumping into the sea. I want a couple of good provocative pieces, everything about him, even down to his shirt size, you understand?

26

Give me the man, the money and his ideals . . . and come back to me before you print any dirt on him, okay? I want another Bob Geldof here, Melissa – no warts, please.'

Melissa clapped her hands together in anticipation. She considered for a second whether or not to kiss him. She decided not. Would Bernard Levin kiss Harold Evans?

Richard Avery. Well, this was one for the scrapbook and no mistake. Melissa thanked Dougherty. Meanwhile, she made a promise to herself to start browsing through the jobs vacant advertisements starting with next Monday's *Guardian*. This call was just a little too close for comfort. And now she might have something worthwhile to put on her CV.

THREE

Charlie had begun with a plan and good intentions. His father had 'absconded' – Charlie's mother's precise word – almost a year ago now. He had been travelling all that time, picking up odd jobs, working his passage from place to place on packet boats and oil tankers. Postcards had arrived from South America, Mexico, Japan, the Arabian Gulf. Charlie would follow his father's progress across the globe in search of . . . what? 'His navel, that's what,' Susan Armstrong would answer drily when asked.

Charlie's own feelings about his father's impulsive departure were ambivalent. He missed him terribly but his longing was made more bearable because of an obscure sense of pride. Charlie approved of his father's adventurousness. However, he also felt the weight of guilt. He blamed himself for driving his father away, although he was never able to explain to himself why.

In the meantime, Charlie had put his plan into action. For every postcard he received from his father Charlie would acquire a fish from that country. However, this strategic plan to develop a United Nations in a fishtank soon crumbled in the face of certain unanticipated practicalities. Charlie's first cruel lesson was that the fact of their all being fish was not a guarantee of brotherly love and peaceful co-existence. Several perished in invisible vendettas. Some found their living conditions lethal while others flourished. Segregation became essential. Fish had little regard for the dimensions of their habitat and produced offspring as if still in the opulent expanse of the Indian Ocean.

Hard choices had to be taken. Some were encouraged to emigrate back to the tropical-fish shop. Charlie's decision had to take account of the available tank space. To be small became an asset. Next, peculiarities of diet were difficult to oblige on Charlie's limited means. A large appetite was a disadvantage.

Dutifully, Charlie consulted the textbooks to discover which varieties were robust yet conscious of their waistlines; which were content with monogamy and moderate in their production of offspring; which were easy-going and sociable. His researches led him to the discovery of computer databases in the United States devoted to fish husbandry. There was a consultant available from the New York Natural History Museum and a computer-linked notice board on which ichthyologists could leave their queries. Charlie immediately saw the need in this country for such a useful service and placed a note on the US bulletin board asking English and European breeders to contact him.

In the past six months Charlie had been contacted by around 120 tropical-fish enthusiasts and was in frequent contact with perhaps two dozen.

Charlie raised the rainbow blind and secured it to two downward-turned S-hooks. His sturdy and graceful fish lived in a highly controlled environment. Every aspect of their sustenance was scrupulously regulated; food supply, water temperature, acidity level, light exposure. The fish liked their twilight world: so did Charlie.

Melissa was browsing through a sheaf of monthly tank bulletins. Charlie recorded everything, even minute fluctuations in water temperature. It was a thoroughness, thought Melissa, verging on fanaticism. She turned and watched as Charlie sprinkled diced food into the two tanks. In the background the printer beat out line after neat line of text. The fanfold paper lifted and glided and tidied itself into a never-ending concertina. It was like watching a slow-motion film of the flapping of a hummingbird's wings. Melissa was impatient for the clackety-clack to finish so they would be able to hear one another.

When the noise ceased Melissa heaved a sigh of relief. She looked at her watch to check the time. Her sister-in-law would be back in about half an hour. If Susan found Melissa at home she would become rigid with anger and start banging cupboard doors in the kitchen until she had left. Susan had chosen to deal with her husband's desertion as if he were a diseased limb that had had to be amputated to prevent further contagion. She regarded Melissa as an hereditary carrier. She hated and resented the easy friendship between her son and his aunt.

'I've come to pick your brains,' Melissa stated bluntly. She told him of the assignment Dougherty had given her. 'There's no way I'm going to digest all this jargon about computers in one day. So, I thought we could come to an agreement.'

'What sort of agreement?' asked Charlie, cautiously.

31

'Well, don't you want to know who I'm interviewing, first?' Charlie sucked his teeth, indifferent. 'Mr Richard Avery, that's who. A computer programmer with knobs on.'

Charlie sat up in his chair. He feigned lack of interest. 'That's nice for you . . . And how can I help?'

Melissa wasn't sure of his reaction and tried to think what else she had to tempt him to help her. If he made any demands she'd offer him lunch at McDonald's as a compromise. 'Well, how would you like to come with me tomorrow when I interview him? If I make a fool of myself you can stop me from putting my foot in my mouth. And if there are things I don't understand about computers, you'd be able to put it in layman's language.'

'Isn't there anyone on the newspaper who can help you?' Charlie was puzzled by her request. He wasn't the only person in the world who understood computer programming. He didn't want to let on yet that he also knew of Avery's connection with the *Sea Shepherd*. Aunt Melissa was nice. But devious.

'I suppose lots of them do, yes,' she answered. 'But I'd like the explanation in words of one syllable.'

'Sure, I'll go with you. Funny thing is,' Charlie laughed, 'I was positive you'd come to ask me about the diver.'

Melissa looked at him quizzically. Her large blue eyes widened. She pouted. 'What diver?'

Charlie tutted. How could someone who was aware of so little ever be a journalist? 'The diver that Daniel and I saw this morning down at Avonmouth. The dead diver. The one that drowned.'

Melissa quickly sucked on her thumb and frowned. 'I don't know anything about a dead diver,' she replied, blankly. 'So tell me what you saw.'

*   *   *   *   *

Professor Kaufmann strode down the corridor. The eggshell gloss paint on the walls absorbed shadows. Galbraith and Hughes followed after him. The pathologist popped the studs of his oil-cloth windcheater as he walked. A faulty ceiling strip light strobed. Kaufmann raised his arm and flicked the starter with his finger as he passed beneath it. The lighting fixture began to hum. The pathologist stretched out his arms and parted the thick rubber door flaps.

He looked back and cautioned, 'Watch the doors. They sometimes swing back. Get a nasty slap in the face if you're not careful.' Hughes pushed open the flap and, ever deferential, stood aside for Galbraith.

The operating theatre reminded Galbraith of his rugby club changing room. The floor and the walls were completely tiled in a dull, mushy pea colour. Small channels crisscrossed the floor; circular drain covers were set in the floor at regular intervals. In the centre of the room lay a three-by-three metre square rubber mattress. This was where the anaesthetised horses and pigs and sheep lay. A veterinarian who had the contract for the Avon Constabulary's dogs and horses had allowed them to use his surgery. In a corner was the metal trolley with the diver's body.

'I just wanted to see if there were any marks or bruises visible on the skin,' explained Galbraith. 'Then I'll get out of your way.'

Kaufmann pushed the trolley directly under one of the ceiling lights.

'There's not a lot I can tell you, Martin,' he said. 'The victim wasn't stabbed and he wasn't shot. But you can see that for yourself. There aren't any signs of violence but, frankly, you wouldn't expect there to be. Not if it was a professional job.'

'I expect not. How long will it take you to do the autopsy?' asked Galbraith casually.

'This'll be a slow one. I'll have to analyse every centimetre of skin tissue for any perforations. You see, he might have been injected. It could take several days to find and still more to analyse the substance. I'm afraid you'll just have to sit it out. But you have my word that I'll work as quickly as possible.'

Kaufmann turned to Galbraith. 'I'm going to tog up. I expect you'd like to get going now. I'll keep you up to date with any findings.'

The telephone rang. Hughes picked up the handset. 'It's the coroner's office,' he informed Galbraith. 'Apparently some reporter on the local paper is inquiring about a dead diver. She's on the line now. The man wants to know what to say to her.'

Galbraith pursed his lips and walked over to the wall telephone. 'This is Galbraith. Put the call through. I'll speak with her.' He waited and heard a few words that gave him his second set-back of the day. However, the woman was just asking for details; he was thankful she knew nothing more. He spoke calmly. 'There is no diver, dead or otherwise, I'm sorry. Have you double-checked your source? . . . Where did the story come from?' She paused and told him it was the usual anonymous phone call. Untraceable, uncontactable, thought Galbraith. 'Sorry, miss. If I do hear anything,

34

shall I call you? What's your name?' He spoke it as she said her name. 'Melissa . . . Nelson. Well, Miss Nelson, I'll let you know if I hear anything.'

* * * * *

It was the first time Richard Avery had visited Galbraith's HQ. What he saw didn't inspire confidence. He looked around the old tobacco warehouse. There still lingered in the air the sweet cloying odour of Virginia leaf. A map of the city was tacked to one wall with different coloured pins dotted here and there. Avery noted that his company's building had a yellow pin head. A trestle table was loaded with electronic equipment including a Revox reel-to-reel tape recorder and a computer monitor that looked a good five years old. Old manual typewriters sat on two office desks that joined together at a right angle.

Hughes had looped the spool of white tape around his wrist like a bracelet. He held the adhesive between his teeth and tore off a strip. He winced as he thought of the pain later when it would be pulled off, tearing hairs from their sockets. The battery was now secured in the well of Avery's back with the little wire aerial riding up the valley between his shoulder blades.

'I'll switch it on now. The batteries have a life of about six hours, that'll be long enough to see you through the evening.'

Avery looked across at Galbraith. He was smoking while he read the evening paper. The Ulsterman was probably in his late thirties, with amber-coloured hair, thinning alarmingly at the temples and the crown. His face, though, showed no trace of the deterioration that his thinning hair suggested. His skin was tight, unlined, with a sharp jawline. He had blue eyes and a boxer's

35

thick nose. Avery found him dour and humourless. It was hard to assess his competence.

Galbraith eventually folded the newspaper and dropped it on the floor. Avery found this casual slovenliness unnerving. It was the gesture of someone who regards where they are as only a temporary resting place, like a bus shelter or an airport lounge. But more than that it brought home to Avery the shabbiness and moral squalor of the operation he was a party to: a plot, a conspiracy, entrapment.

When Nestor Greffen, a small-time businessman of Eastern European origins, had come to him three months ago with his proposal, Avery had waited a day and then contacted the police. A meeting had been arranged with a Mr Nicholson in nearby Bath. Over lunch Nicholson, correct, scrupulously discreet and as cold as a tortoise, had suggested Avery appear to co-operate with Greffen's plan. Nicholson confirmed that Greffen was not known to have contacts with Soviet agents. It was his suspicion, he confided, that Greffen's somewhat unorthodox approach suggested an opportunist, a maverick. Greffen, he thought, was a small-time hustler trying for a scoop. He had bitten off more than he could chew.

Things had dramatically escalated several days later. Greffen and Avery had met a second time, and this time Greffen offered Avery an envelope as he bid goodbye. Inside was a photograph of a young girl, perhaps thirteen years old. In fact, precisely thirteen years and four months old, Avery calculated. For the girl in the picture was his daughter, his own child, whom he had never seen and scarcely ever thought

36

about. But she existed; she was real. Avery needed no more proof than this black and white snap.

Immediately, Avery contacted Nicholson again. In three days Galbraith and his surveillance outfit had materialised. The operation had assumed a momentum of its own. At the outset Avery had been the axis, the focal point. He saw himself at the centre of the spider's web. But he had been mistaken. Now he knew he was no more than a mere paste stone in some wizardly jeweller's fantastic confection. He was the counterfeit bauble. His task was both to attract and deceive. It did not flatter him.

In other ways, though, this reduction of his role seemed appropriate. For the sudden reappearance of his daughter had at once stimulated a profound guilt. He had almost completely suppressed the memory of her. His soul craved punishment. He was a father who had utterly disregarded his own flesh and blood. His conscience tormented him. Nevertheless, he was keenly aware that his acute suffering was only mental. He could not erase from his mind the awful emotional and physical neglect he had inflicted on his unacknowledged daughter. He was prepared to pay almost any penance.

Avery glanced at Galbraith sucking on his cigarette and expelling the smoke through his nostrils. He wondered if this was his nemesis, this Ulsterman in whom contempt crackled like boiling sugar. Galbraith returned the stare, undaunted. 'I lost my diver,' he said hoarsely, addressing Avery. 'The man I sent down to have a peek at that boat of yours.'

Avery looked down at the tails of his open shirt and

37

began closing the buttons. He knew Galbraith was laying the blame for this on his shoulders. It was irrational and yet just.

'So . . . ?' he replied. He would not pretend to offer his condolences; that would be hypocrisy.

Galbraith didn't seem to expect more. 'So. So don't play silly buggers with Greffen this evening. Act as natural as you can. Play it as if you're completely on your own.'

'I always do,' replied Avery, his voice tempered with a chilling frankness.

*　　*　　*　　*　　*

— You need a brandy, Richard.

— Everything seemed to be going so well.

— It still is. It's a stressful time for you.

— You're not joking.

— You're anxious. That's quite natural.

— I'm glad you noticed.

— But you have to use it. Make it work for you, not against you.

— Not any longer, Nestor. They're on to something.

— Oh, I doubt that, Richard . . . The diver? . . . One lousy diver. Come. That's minimum surveillance. Possibly he had time to hook up a limpet mike. Frankly, I doubt it. If he was as bad a workman as he was a diver, we're home and dry. In a manner of speaking.

— You're taking it very casually.

— I see no reason to become agitated. They've obviously given it such a low priority they got some diver out of retirement. They're interested in the *Sea Shepherd*. Don't tell me you didn't expect to attract their attention?

— No. Of course I expected something.

— And now you've got it. And a damp squib it turned out to be, though it gives me great joy to say I told you so. They ran the operation exactly as we predicted. To tell you the truth, we wouldn't have people like that allowed to inspect bus tickets.

Tony Hughes shifted listlessly on the hard wooden bench. His eyes remained fixed, watching the aluminium platters of the tape deck turn slowly. A speaker amplified the conversation.

He stretched his back and jiggled his spine. He had brought along a small grip-bag with a thermos of coffee. A refreshment machine was about the only technological instrument the converted TV detector van lacked. He poured out the steaming brown liquid in the metal cap that doubled as a cup. He made a gesture, offering some to his boss. But Galbraith did not deign to notice the friendly gesture.

Beside him, Galbraith was motionless. It was almost as if he were listening to God reciting his final judgement. The balance sheet was exhaustive and ruthless. Galbraith would be lucky to get away with two millennia in purgatory and 36,000 novenas. Hughes checked himself. He was being uncharitable. As a good Catholic he knew that he should abstain from throwing the first stone. He was not without blemish himself. But he instinctively withdrew his charitableness from zealots like Galbraith. Then, an uncomfortable thought occurred to him: was Galbraith Protestant? Or, perhaps, was he a Catholic like himself who had obvious reasons for concealing his faith?

39

Hughes paused in his ruminations and judged himself harshly. Only God could see into men's souls. Greffen was certainly not God. On the contrary, he was the Devil. 'Lord, how dumb I am,' a silent voice in his head chided. Suddenly, he realised that he had unwittingly succumbed to Greffen's sweet-tasting poison. For Greffen was following step by step Chapter One of the tradecraft manual. It was basic stuff, straightforward disinformation, drawn straight from the KGB vaults. Greffen was carefully sowing the seeds of doubt and distrust in Avery's mind.

Hughes tried to remember the procedure. Make the subject distance himself psychologically from his own side by denigrating their professional ability. And cut away the escape route before he even thinks of using it. Always assume your recruit is a double agent. Make him understand the positive advantages of working solely for you, show him gratitude from us and thanklessness from them. Pay him compliments while describing their ingratitude. Show your side to be a huge and well-informed and efficient organisation that proceeds cautiously but acts decisively. Paint the opposition as a multi-headed hydra tripping itself on its uncoordinated feet which can only be a liability to your recruit. Make him see that he is indispensable to us while a potential and disposable embarrassment to them. It was pure textbook. Hughes coughed with shame at his gullibility and warm coffee dribbled over his foolscap clipboard.

Tuning his mind back to the distant conversation, he noted that Galbraith had not allowed his attention to be distracted for a second. His admiration suddenly grew. Galbraith, after all, hadn't missed a trick. He'd even foreseen Greffen's manoeuvre and had Avery wired with a microphone so that he could later undo Greffen's invisible manacles.

— I think we should postpone. At least until another route out can be found.
— Richard ... Richard ... Have someone do a routine hull inspection in the morning. Will that reassure you? Listen to me. Listen to me. They'll drop it now and amuse themselves with an inquiry.
— How can you be so confident?
— I know what these sort of people are like. They're small-minded, careful, like insurance clerks. Believe me, someone is already working overtime thinking up an excuse to save his boss's neck.
— I want out. If it's impossible to postpone, I'm out. We cancel everything.
— I can't allow that. I wouldn't even dare suggest such a thing to my superiors. You understand? ... I wouldn't dare ... And besides, we have already put our side of the deal into action.
— What do you mean?
— I mean your daughter. She's on her way to England at this moment.
— ...
— What is it?
— But what if ...
— What if what? ...
— If I ...
— If I were in your shoes, Richard, I'd be hoping

41

we won't be as careless with the little girl as they
were with their diver. That's what I'd be hoping.

—   ....
....
....

Galbraith swung round in annoyance. 'Damn this
fancy stupid equipment. And damn your batteries, too,
Hughes.'

FOUR

Melissa smiled conspiratorially at Charlie over the roof of the car. As she locked the door she noticed that she was still wearing her sheepskin house slippers. Perfect footwear, she thought, for stealthy work.

They took the lift from the underground carpark to the second floor of her office building. The main newsroom and editorial offices were on this floor with accounts and administration on the third. As there was no morning edition of the paper Melissa did not expect to find anyone working after 8 p.m. Her intuition was right; everyone had gone home. She led Charlie to her desk, and looked expectantly at the Sainsbury's carrier bag.

'I'm counting on you,' she whispered.

'Don't get your hopes up too high,' he replied.

Charlie laid the plastic bag delicately on the table top and took out a box. Quickly, expertly he began coupling the cables between Melissa's desktop computer and his own telephone modem. The modem was an ugly but sophisticated box of tricks that made computer to computer conversation possible via the normal telephone lines. They were going to try and raid the National Police Computer for information on the drowned diver who had now vanished without trace. Charlie had insisted the risky operation should be done from her office.

Charlie had acquired the confidential telephone number from a generous but anonymous hacker donor. Such things were not unusual. Hackers were inveterate scavengers, for ever collecting tidbits of information. The most mouth-watering delicacy, for them, was a private database telephone number. However, though they might be scavengers they were not hoarders: hackers always obeyed their unwritten code of ethics and were most diligent in seeing to the widest distribution of their prized nuggets of digits.

Charlie's own bulletin board had a very limited clientele: fellow tropical-fish enthusiasts. Nevertheless, he was a member of the brotherhood of hackers and though he rarely had anything to offer he was never forgotten. When, recently, the National Police Computer telephone number had scrolled across his screen he made a note of it – for a rainy day. He now called it up and the welcoming logo asked him to type in his identity password.

'We're not getting anything, are we?' Melissa asked impatiently.

Charlie looked at the screen, his features puckering with the effort of concentration and frustration.

'Except maybe a short stay in prison,' he replied with irritation. 'I can't do any more without a password.'

'Why don't you try "Hello, hello, hello . . .",' Melissa suggested facetiously.

Melissa was bearing down on Charlie, looking over his shoulder. Her close proximity intimidated him. Illogically, he felt guilty for not being able to penetrate

44

the system and satisfy Melissa. This disturbed him more than the real illegality of the actual action he was engaged in.

'It's best not to keep the line open for too long. Makes it easier to trace.'

Melissa was reluctant to admit defeat at such an early moment. But she had to acknowledge that it was pointless prolonging the risk. She was never going to overcome this obstacle.

'Okay,' she sighed, 'turn the blessed thing off.'

'I'm sorry, Melissa.' Charlie tried to find some words to dispel her gloom. 'You see, it's what we call a "dead entry". That means we've managed to get in but no further.'

Melissa lashed out with sudden anger. 'You people even have technical words for a shambles.'

They were both silent. Melissa pulsed with an angry frustration that could not locate its target. Charlie was numbed by the unexpected venom. Melissa heaved a sigh.

'They invent words only to conceal their meaning,' she said enigmatically. Charlie looked blank. 'It makes me mad, this obsession with secrecy. A man died – that diver – and it's not enough for them. They try to erase his existence totally. Why? *Why?*'

Charlie switched the computer on again. 'I've tried all the ways I can think of. We'll have one more go.'

Melissa drummed her fingers on the tabletop. She took a few steps and looked out of the window to the city below. A group of youths eating chips and fried chicken and two old men were standing in front of the plateglass window of a television showroom watching a snooker championship on a dozen television sets. In the background three TV screens displayed Prestel and Ceefax. The bluish ciphers of video recorders flashed off and on. We are innocent infants, Melissa reflected, beguiled by toys. She turned and looked at Charlie toiling with the intractable machine.

'Don't think I'm blaming you, Charlie. It's not you I'm angry with. It's this technology, these contraptions . . . all they've done is make the fences invisible. They haven't torn them down, they've just replaced them.The powerful have managed to reinforce their barricades. And the rest of us connive at the deception. We've slowly lost our appetite for knowledge and replaced it with the craving to be entertained.'

She collected her raincoat and wrapped her lambswool scarf around her shoulders. It was time to leave. Melissa felt like railing against the world. Her thoughts made her hungry for activity, for some little act of rebellion. She experienced a misanthropic distaste for humankind that had squandered its human rights.

'Let's call it a night,' she told Charlie. He began uncoupling the cables and wires, winding them round his fist, securing them with rubber bands. Newspapers are nothing more now than a Punch and Judy show for the punters. A lucky dip, a fairground sideshow. Melissa reminded herself that she had gladly accepted to plunge her hands up to her elbows inside the puppet. She had pledged to do her best to enchant and distract the punter. Now she vowed to herself that she would get to the bottom of this diver story. She would redeem her honour by making her piece on Richard Avery one thing of which she could be proud.

*　　*　　*　　*　　*

46

Simultaneously, two pneumatic drills started to tear at the pavement. It was 8.30 a.m.

Susan Armstrong turned up the volume on the radio to compete with the noise from the street. Although it was half term, she estimated Charlie would be downstairs demanding breakfast in another five minutes. She rubbed her eyes and caught her reflection in one of the window panes. She had thick and indomitably straight hair cut in Japanese style, geometric, with a hennaed fringe. She had always been conscious of her full lips and excused them from lipstick. Besides, her complexion was fresh and didn't need embellishing with cosmetics.

Susan had quickly reinstated her maiden name when her husband Peter left. She could not be sure that his departure was definitive but that hardly mattered. To continue being referred to as Mrs Nelson was painful and pointless. Each time a sales assistant returned her account card the 'Thank you, Mrs Nelson' made her skin tingle and her heart ache. She felt like an impostor. She thought people would note her strange reaction and alert the store detectives thinking she had stolen the card. One by one she had removed her husband's invisible presence from bank cards, electricity bills, motor insurance premiums. It was a drawn-out amputation that required of her the steely resolve that is supposed to come naturally to an officer's daughter.

Her parents had nurtured in her the idea that marriage was as solid and permanent an institution as Crosse and Blackwell or Benson and Hedges. Around her, as she was growing up, families flourished in the Gloucestershire villages. She could understand now, with hindsight, that there had been tensions stretched

47

to breaking point of which she had never been aware. Also, among farmers and those who lived on the land, divorce or separation struck a mortal economic blow. If a marriage collapsed so, too, did the family's farm or dairy. In those days anyway, only twenty years ago, divorce was a misfortune that blighted only city folk.

Life in the country had taught Susan the advantage of having a hobby. There were few distractions after school. Her parents had resisted television until the late 1960s when colour arrived and they were able to enjoy the glistening hues on the flanks of horseflesh in 'The Horse Of The Year Show'. Susan, meanwhile, had become fascinated with the newly invented Polaroid instant camera.

She turned her attention back to the glass photo plates in the sink and scrubbed them with increased vigour. She had picked them up at a country auction as a job lot. The bromide film had become tacky and congealed. Some of them were now inseparable, locked face to face forever. Fortunately, the majority were only coated with a stubborn resin of dust. She would scrub the non-emulsion sides and then put them in the dishwasher. A sixty per cent recovery rate seemed guaranteed.

She held up one of the glass plates drying in the wire dishrack, and looked at the negative image. She was able to make out a strong middle-aged man in a vulcanised overall standing on a small pier with a fishing boat in the background. He was flanked by two younger men who had draped their fishing net over their shoulders. It made them look like a pair of Roman courtiers in togas who had cheated time and material-ised in the last quarter of the nineteenth century. It was as if the world had, for a moment, slipped its axis in this anonymous image. And doubly so, since the fisherman in the centre himself would soon be catapulted forward in time when Susan produced a new print from it. The old fisherman would find a world where candour was as rare as a unicorn. We have double-glazed our minds, Susan thought. We have lagged our hearts so the warmth cannot leak out.

Over the patter-patter of the synchronised power drills Susan heard Charlie's feet on the stairs. 'I'll make some breakfast, shall I?' she shouted out.

'It's okay, Mum. I'm off out now. Don't bother.'

Susan laid the glass photo plate carefully on the steel draining board. She scraped the rubber gloves off her hands as she ascended the stairs to the ground floor. Charlie stood on the chessboard tiles admiring his outfit in the hall mirror. Susan noticed a postcard on the rattan table along with some brown manilla envelopes. The post had brought another card from Charlie's father.

'There's a card from Dad. Look's like he's back in Sri Lanka. Do you want to read it?'

Susan smarted. She replied stiffly, 'I don't read other people's correspondence.' She opened the front room door. 'Can you give me a minute, darling, before you go?' The room was Susan's office-cum-showroom. Its walls were densely crowded with sombre black and white prints in black varnished frames. Charlie followed her in.

Susan studied her son's face. But he had already assumed the glazed expression of the wrongly accused which immediately advertises guilt.

'I'm not a nagging mother, Charlie. God knows, I

don't make many demands. I appreciate that when you're young you need to feel independent.' Susan had thought that she should begin with a tone that set them as equals and would allow Charlie the opportunity to make his admission before charges were pressed. She knew instantly that her tactfulness was wasted. Charlie stared at her. He would say nothing to incriminate himself.

Susan forsook diplomacy. 'I know Melissa was here yesterday, Charlie. I smelt that perfume she wears. And I suppose you're going off to meet her now. It's certainly not Daniel you're seeing dressed like that. You know I draw the line at Melissa. I don't like you seeing her.'

Charlie was only mildly stubborn. 'I know you don't make lots of rules, Mum,' he said evenly. 'But Melissa is my aunt. She's part of my family even if you don't like her. She's Dad's sister.'

Susan knew that nothing she could say would shake his resolve to maintain this relationship. Susan had never liked Melissa, even during the early trouble-free years of her marriage. She had watched Melissa evolve from a precocious teenager into a manipulative and hard-edged woman.

'Well, I don't like her,' said Susan weakly.

'And I do,' countered Charlie emphatically. 'She's showing me what a journalist does. She's helping me, teaching me.'

There was no middle ground for them to meet on and hope of reaching a compromise. When his father went away Charlie had found a huge portion of his emotions stranded in limbo. Gradually, he had shifted these loose, rootless emotions on to Melissa. Susan was sure that Melissa would sever them once more as abruptly as her brother had done. Susan was trying to protect him from more anguish. But her protection appeared to him like jealousy.

'Don't be naïve, Charlie. The only person she's helping is herself.'

Charlie remembered last night at the newspaper office and the way Melissa had urged him to persist with the raid on the police computer. But his mother knew nothing about that; she was simply surmising.

'You're just prejudiced.'

'I know what she's like . . . she uses people. Be warned. I don't want you getting involved in any of her schemes.'

'She doesn't have any schemes.' Charlie turned away and snapped the door shut behind him.

FIVE

— If I were in your shoes, Richard, I'd be hoping
we won't be as careless with the little girl as they
were with their diver. That's what I'd be hoping.

Galbraith arched back in his chair and raised his hand
to switch on the light. The fluorescent strip quivered
and flashed. Galbraith grimaced. Francis Nicholson
held his palm over his eyes to accustom them slowly
to the sudden surge of intense light after the dark.

Tony Hughes marked a line across his notebook. He
believed in always having to hand a meticulous record
of any meeting. It was a practice he had acquired in
the police and it was his experience that there were
always as many versions of a meeting as there were
people in it. Besides, this current operation was
extremely accident-prone; his notes would be his
insurance when the dam burst.

He reached across the table and switched off the slide
projector. 'I'm afraid that's the point when Avery's
battery packed in, sir,' he informed Nicholson. 'We
have nothing more on tape.'

'No,' agreed Nicholson. He had broken a short out-of-season holiday at his cottage in Aldeburgh to return and take charge. His assessment of Nestor Greffen, he realised, had been wildly optimistic and mistaken. He was certain now that Greffen was the type of agent known as a 'sleeper'. He had arrived in England and settled here over twenty-two years ago. In that time he had never had any contacts with communist agents under the department's surveillance. This was the normal practice with a sleeper. He had also built up a business which absolved him of the need to collect sums of money either in person or through banks or any other traceable way. His operation was also self-financing. This, too, was usual practice. Nicholson relished the irony: communist agents were often obliged to become capitalist entrepreneurs in order to maintain their cover identities. But, in espionage, there were many ironies.

'Mr Galbraith,' Nicholson enunciated roundly. 'You are in frequent contact with Richard Avery. What is your reading of these events?'

Galbraith had known he would be asked for the overview. In his opinion Greffen had smelt bad from the start, like a rotten egg inside a healthy shell. He surmised that there was more to Avery than he had been told; certainly more than Nicholson himself knew.

'Well,' he began carefully, 'I think it's pretty clear now that Greffen is signalling to Avery that he holds all the trumps. First, we learn that he has produced this long lost daughter from thin air. So he's telling Avery he's working on behalf of whatever country she lives in. He isn't the one-man show we reckoned him to be. Second . . . there's our unfortunate diver. He doesn't have to say in so many words that he gave the

54

order to kill him for Avery to pick up the message.' He paused. 'Greffen has now got a carrot and a stick. The daughter is the carrot. And the threat of violence is the stick.'

'Yes, indeed.' Nicholson ruminated. His eyes were strangely still. He didn't blink. He was like a lizard basking. His jaw rose and dropped as he made chewing motions. 'And do we know the results of the post mortem on our diver man yet, Hughes?'

Hughes sat up and crossed one hand over the other on the table like a television newsreader. 'I'm sorry. I'm afraid not.' He leaned forward and wet his lips. 'We are breathing down their necks, though,' he offered warmly.

Hughes was the type of man Nicholson felt most comfortable with. He understood perfectly the polite and affable stonewalling, but this morning he was not in the mood for it.

'You're not on oath at an inquest, Hughes. Give me an educated guess. Was he pushed . . . or did he fall?'

Galbraith observed their easy familiarity. They could be father and son. Same class, same top drawer. He felt sudden contempt for their cosiness.

'It's hard to say really, sir.' Hughes looked straight at Nicholson so that his superior could see sincerity glisten in his eyes.

'Then let me cross the t's and dot the i's for you both,' Nicholson said crisply. 'If the diver was killed on Greffen's orders then we must fear for the safety of Richard Avery. And the girl, too. There are other lives at risk and I will not put them into jeopardy simply to get a result in this operation. Is that understood?'

Galbraith jutted his chin forward. 'Yes, sir.'

Tony Hughes became serious, adjusting in his chameleon-like manner to the sudden change in atmosphere. Nicholson pushed back his chair and rose to leave. Hughes coughed.

'There is something else, though. Some journalist seems to have found out about the diver. She said the report came from a tip-off from a member of the public.'

So, Galbraith said to himself, this is the little treacherous egg Hughes has been hatching all morning. Galbraith had already dealt with that one. It was so minor it wasn't worth mentioning. But Hughes, unctuous and boyscoutish, had dropped it in at the last moment.

Nicholson flushed with anger. His thin lips froze. 'I presume you have at least dealt with *that* matter,' he said glowering at Galbraith.

It was not yet lunchtime and, Nicholson lamented, a routine little surveillance had escalated into a devilishly intricate web of deception and needless killing. He had only guided Avery gently into pursuing his contact with Greffen because he thought Greffen might evolve into an interesting vessel. Now it was as clear as day that Greffen was Soviet gold ore that had been hidden away in the back seams of Bristol society for over twenty years. The man had not spat on a pavement or double parked or been late with his rates once in all that time. When one thought about it, of course, he did seem too good to be true. He hadn't cost his masters a penny. Indeed, they probably had a return on the investment. He was gold; and his value had increased a thousand fold. But he was their gold and not ours.

*   *   *   *   *

Charlie waited for Melissa in the piazza. He gazed into the ornamental pool where disconsolate goldfish mooched around listlessly. They had to make their homes among the debris of careless citizens who deposited empty drinks cans, crumpled cigarette packages and yawning styrofoam hamburger cases. Some had already died because of the unhealthy living conditions. Who on earth, Charlie wondered, had the bright idea of populating a busy precinct pool with live fish? It was insensitive, callous.

Melissa beeped her car horn. Charlie took a last glance at the fishpond and jogged over to the kerb.

'Fit and ready?' she asked brightly. 'All set for twenty questions with Mr Richard Avery?'

She opened the door and Charlie folded himself into the front passenger seat. Straightaway, Melissa noticed something subdued in his demeanour. 'What's the matter?'

Charlie pouted. 'Mum. She got on at me this morning about seeing you. You know how you stir her up.'

Melissa raised her eyebrows. 'Why did you tell her if you knew how she'd react?'

'I didn't tell her. She said she smelt your perfume,' Charlie replied candidly. But Melissa winced.

Susan was a subject Melissa did not want to cloud the day ahead over. They snapped themselves into the seatbelts and Melissa revved up before slipping the handbrake. She enjoyed the litheness of her car, its power, and derived satisfaction from daring manoeuvres in traffic. She liked to execute dainty little lane shifts and sudden bursts of speed and watch the tormented expressions on the faces of her meek fellow motorists.

Things were buzzing in her head. She had worked hard digging for background on Avery and unearthed some details which tantalised her. She was eager to share them with Charlie. First, however, she brought him up to date on her fruitless inquiry into the dead and now vanished diver.

'There's no smoke without fire,' she began, and went on to tell Charlie the series of events that had happened when she arrived at work that morning. Her editor, Bernard Dougherty, usually a lamb, was transformed into a dragon breathing fire. Somehow, Melissa explained, he had found out that she knew of the diver and was asking around. 'Well, he'd really had the wind put up him. Told me to lay off, said he dished out the stories, I took what I was given and if I didn't like it . . . la-de-da and so on.' Melissa said she reckoned Dougherty's usually talkative sergeant at the central police station had told him to lay off this one without going into precise reasons.

'Dougherty's such a patsy anyway,' said Melissa disloyally. 'He was made to be pushed around.' One thing that went without saying, though, was Dougherty wasn't going to bite the hand that fed him. The police gave him lots of leads and stories, they made up half the news in the paper, and Dougherty obviously feared his well might dry up if Melissa poked around any further on this diver business.

'The message was clearly, "Lay off, or you're going to kill the goose that lays the golden eggs",' Melissa concluded succinctly.

'Well, I guess that's the end of that, then.'

'Hardly,' said Melissa, surprised at Charlie's willingness to yield so quickly. 'The thing is, there *must* be a diver and there must be some very weird goings on. Otherwise why go to all this trouble trying to bury the story? No smoke without fire, you see?'

Melissa asked Charlie to summarise, as simply as possible, quite what aspect of the computer business Richard Avery was involved in.

'Didn't they teach you anything about computers at school?' Charlie moaned.

'Fortunately, neither boys nor computers were invented when I was at school. All we learned was how to bake griddle scones,' Melissa riposted tartly. '. . . and karate,' she added with a menacing look.

'A database is really a big computer filled with information files,' he began deliberately. 'Avery's company sells protection systems to prevent people who shouldn't from getting into the big computer. I mean it's real complicated stuff when you get into system design and all that. But it's that simple.'

'Thank you,' Melissa chirped. 'That's just what I thought.'

Melissa left the outer ring road and joined the slow moving stream of traffic filtering on to the A4. The journey to Avery's house would take them along the Bath road. Just before reaching the city itself they would fork off on to a country lane and meander through the Wiltshire countryside. Probably sitting on the tail of a tractor, Melissa forecast bleakly, for five winding miles.

Avery, she discovered, had got into computer programming years ago, at a time when it was still thought to be as barmy and exotic as naturism. He had seen the future and knew it worked. All companies have to maintain files and keep records of their products, customers, sales, personnel, finances. Larger companies have more files and so more people to create them and manage them. Computers would allow these companies to maintain these files but reduce the personnel needed to administer them. If one obstacle could be overcome: the obstacle was security. Not everyone who needed access to the files should have the capacity to see every file. Some were confidential, some were not. If a computer programme could be devised to discriminate between users so that the system itself granted authority to the user, every company that used computers would want such a programme. The larger the company the greater their need, Avery reasoned. So he went after the multinationals – the car manufacturers, steel companies, aircraft industries, munitions, food giants.

Melissa was appalled at how rich the man must be. Especially galling was the fact that Avery hadn't started with money. He was a regular Bristol grammar school boy who had the gift of reading the future. His wealth would have been more acceptable if it were inherited. Then, at least, Melissa could have felt her dislike of his fortune fully justified. She resented people who succeeded on brains alone; it was an affront to a brainy person like herself. 'If him, then why not me?'

Avery was unusual in another respect. He was a scientist with a conscience. Melissa was amazed to find out that when he was a student reading physics at university he had waded waist-high into left politics. This also contradicted the image she expected of him, and she was angry with him for contradicting her. It made her seem small-minded. She wanted a cigar-puffing ex-public school snob who ground his workers with the heel of his shiny capitalist's boot. Instead, the man was a radical, a student activist, an enlightened employer, who even provided an on-site crèche free for his employees and gave maternity leave to both mothers and fathers. And a conservationist. It was too good to be true! Melissa knew, instinctively, that all that glitters is not gold. There had to be a scandal. Somewhere.

Melissa drummed her foot on the accelerator, punishing her car for her own frustration. Charlie was irritating, too. He was convinced Avery was Sir Bountiful, a philanthropist, almost a saint. Melissa tried to restrain Charlie's enthusiasm.

'I know what he's doing with the *Sea Shepherd* seems worthwhile to you, protecting the environment and all that,' she began, appearing to give Avery the benefit of her doubt before she blackened his name, 'but first and foremost he's a businessman, Charlie. People like him don't usually believe in doing something for nothing. Believe me, there's more to him than meets the eye. The only saints these days are made of plaster.'

A couple of minutes later the car bumped over the cattle grid at the main gate. Melissa slowed down for a few seconds, considering the splendid eighteenth-century gabled stone mansion with its chalk-white tapering pillars. 'Such perfect taste,' she muttered to herself.

SIX

Melissa accelerated as she approached the hairpin bend at the front entrance of the house. She threw on the brakes and chips of gravel flew into the air.

The kitchen had migrated from the back of the house. It now occupied the front west wing, giving the cook a view of rolling parklands and copses to stimulate her culinary creations. The crunching of tyres on gravel alerted Rachel to the arrival of Mr Avery's luncheon guest. She picked up her distance glasses and held them in front of her eyes. Rachel was the housekeeper; a loyal, grey-haired woman who prevented the outside world from intruding on Richard Avery's domestic tranquillity. Her jaw dropped.

Rachel drew apart the panoramic sliding glass windows and scuttled out of the kitchen onto the terrace.

'There's two of you!' she exclaimed, her voice rising with surprise.

'Yes,' Melissa answered calmly.

'Your son?' Rachel queried. She had dedicated herself to terminating Avery's bachelorhood. Rachel reviewed carefully each new young woman she came across as a potential candidate. Her first questions were always aimed at establishing the young woman's civil status.

'No. Nephew.'

Rachel's eyes sparkled. 'I'll set an extra place,' she added with satisfaction.

Rachel opened the high front door and showed the pair into the hall. A wide staircase swept down into the centre of the marble flagged reception area which was decorated with Chinese lacquer chests and potted ferns.

'This way, please,' indicated Rachel, opening a door padded in green leather like a Chesterfield sofa. She showed them into Avery's ground-floor library. Rachel closed the door and went in search of Mr Avery. Melissa examined the room with envious eyes. Her hand stroked the leather cushions of a sofa which, she thought to herself, probably cost as much as she made in a year. The door opened and Avery entered the room, his hand outstretched.

'I'm pleased you were able to come out here to see me, Miss Nelson. It's so much more informal than at my office.' He shook first Melissa's hand and then Charlie's, firmly. He smiled at Charlie. 'Rachel tells me this is your nephew. But you seem too young to have a nephew who's almost a grown man.' He managed to flatter both of them simultaneously.

Melissa explained that Charlie had come along as her walking reference book; she was unfamiliar with virtually every aspect of computer jargon. Avery proposed a tour of the house and led them up the staircase to the first floor. Melissa noted that, although formal and elegant, the pictures and furnishings suggested a highly personal choice. Avery had not, as she had expected, simply hired a decorator to equip the place wholesale. It was homely and friendly despite its size and its meagre two inhabitants.

Avery was relaxed. He placed his hands on Charlie's shoulder when he pointed out a plaster relief on the ceiling and explained the significance of the figures. They represented the husband and wife who had commissioned the house more than 200 years ago. Avery commented that he found it poignant that their love should have endured so long and inspired the subsequent dwellers. Melissa used this as a cue to inquire why Avery himself had never married.

'I'm afraid I failed to take advantage when the opportunity was there,' he confessed frankly. 'Marriage had rather fallen out of fashion when I was in my early twenties. People just lived together; to get married was to sell out and place yourself on the side of convention. I didn't want a bourgeois life, or so I thought then.'

He went on to describe the circumstances of his first involvement in the computer software business. He noticed Melissa grimace when he mentioned deals and mergers and expansion.

'I think, Miss Nelson,' Avery continued, 'you've got the wrong idea about me. I wasn't cut out to be just another businessman or entrepreneur. It's not money that interests me, not even power. Maybe I'm flattering myself, but I've always tried to be a pioneer, an explorer . . . I've always come in at the frontier, and then gone beyond it.'

Melissa felt he was a little too eager to justify himself, give her the Mr Nice Guy flannel. Everyone lusted after money, everyone was thirsty for power. She suspected his last speech had been scripted for him by some firm of publicity image-makers and he was reciting it by rote. Her speculations were cut short by the shrill beeping of a telephone paging device. Melissa and Avery reached together into their pockets.

'I think it must be for you,' Avery said, glancing at his own messenger. He opened the bedroom door for her. 'There's a telephone in here you can use.'

Richard Avery sighed with some relief. He disliked giving interviews. He was not a person who found nourishment in public notoriety or fame. Besides, the portrayal of him as some micro-electronic wizard only disguised the fact that he had built up his business with desperate effort. His was not an overnight success story. He was pleased Charlie was there, it was an opportunity to switch into another gear.

He guided Charlie downstairs to the living room. 'Are you fond of fish?' he asked, opening the double doors.

Charlie held his face about ten centimetres from the aquarium. His eyes blinked. He studied the languid fish and tried to read their mute conversations. Their lips opened and closed rhythmically. Charlie admired the Mosaic Gourami with its delicate ventral rays. The fish was dappled with pearl-like spots against the brown body. Its fin-rays were like delicate lace doilies. The electric blue mouth of a Jack Dempsey hove into view and the fish rotated sideways, asking to be admired. He was quite large and his body shimmered with greenish blue spots like a hand-worked brass bowl. His flesh was quite dark.

'That's a great gourami,' said Charlie with authority. 'But you're taking a real chance keeping a Jack

Dempsey in there with him,' he added with a note of caution. 'A Jack Dempsey will eat him for breakfast.'

Richard Avery smiled. He was impressed. 'He was the first fish I ever bought,' he explained. 'But he's a very old fellow now; there's not much fight left in him. He gets along with the others, he likes the company.' Charlie now turned and inspected the imposing room.

'You really do know something about fish, Charlie,' remarked Avery, encouraging Charlie to explore this second common link between them.

Charlie explained how he had started his collection of tropical fish. He told Avery of the postcards he received from his father from the Far East and other tropical places. When Avery asked whether his father brought the fish back home with him, Charlie stated simply that he hadn't been home for a long time and probably wouldn't be back for many years.

Richard Avery noted a certain timbre in Charlie's voice. It was neither exactly sadness nor even, as he might have expected, bitterness. It was, strangely, with a mixture of yearning and admiration that he spoke of his father; and affectionate nostalgia.

'And the fish remind you of him?' Avery guessed.

'I suppose so,' offered Charlie. 'Yes,' he agreed.

Charlie described how he had set up his computer notice board for the exchange of information and news on tropical fish. He detailed how calls had come in from fellow ichthyologists in Japan, New Zealand and the USA and that there was now a regular newsletter sent from a researcher who worked at the Museum of Natural History in New York.

As he listened, Avery became aware of the boy's

compassion. It was a further bond between them. The two of them were concerned to protect the natural world, to defend both creatures and environment from short-sighted exploitation and commercial abuse. But, Avery noted too, Charlie found a contentment in his gentle nursing of tropical fish that was an important substitute for the tender feelings he was not able to share with his absent father.

When, over lunch, Melissa had suggested that Avery's sponsorship of the *Sea Shepherd* and his attempts to publicise the damage caused by toxic waste to the sea and its creatures was nothing more than a public relations gimmick, Avery reacted angrily. He knew only too well that the press thought they had a duty to denigrate and slur with their cynicism all efforts to improve the world. Journalists never seemed able to recognise simple humanity.

'It doesn't matter to me what people think of me,' he began. 'What matters is that they are made aware of the threat to our world and do something about it. There are millions of people as concerned as I am. We're just doing whatever is within our means to do. If my means are greater, then so should be my contribution. I'm doing no more than that. People can say what they like. I shan't give up just to satisfy their small-mindedness.'

Melissa saw his flashing anger and, prudently, refrained from speaking, serving herself instead a Bath Oliver biscuit. Charlie beamed with pride at Avery's defence of what Melissa termed 'do-gooders'. There was an uncomfortable tension in the air for some moments. Rachel returned from the kitchen carrying a tray with little white porcelain pots.

'It's chocolate mousse,' she announced. 'I only made two,' she whispered apologetically.

Melissa sipped her sugarless black coffee from a bell-shaped cup with an ornate gold leaf design. Avery was distracting Charlie with a sleek micro in his office. Charlie was mesmerised by a paintbox programme with which he transformed the colours of a cubist painting from magenta to cobalt blue to sunflower yellow and back again.

She watched the two of them amusing themselves. The computer enthralled them as much as a Scalextric or train set used to thrill Charlie's father when they were children. Melissa thought she might avail herself of Avery's preoccupation to ask him some questions. She turned a leaf in her notebook and glanced downwards.

'But aren't you concerned that your radical opinions could jeopardise your company?' she inquired.

Avery looked across at her. He was too careful a businessman to blurt out inadvertently an unconsidered thought.

'I don't have radical opinions,' he answered with an ingenuous grin.

'But as a student you were on the broad left,' Melissa continued.

He felt as though he had been punched in the chest. His heart pounded. His face flushed with anger. But he quickly restored his mood to its habitual placid calm. He spoke to her with a bluff frankness hoping it concealed his surprise.

'It was nothing more than a youthful flirtation, an adolescent romance. Being rebellious is natural at that

69

age,' he assured her, as if it were no more serious than admitting to having once broken a window with a football.

Melissa scented his anxiety, though. She was determined to probe further; her appetite was whetted. She smiled quickly to disarm him, then consolidated her advantage.

'You even made several journeys to Iron Curtain countries' – she read her notes – 'Cuba in 1969, Hungary and Poland in 1970.'

Avery came from behind the desk and stood facing her in the centre of the room. He was no longer the fatherly friend letting a kid have a go on his new toy. He immediately became the rich and powerful man implied by these surroundings.

He gazed unflinchingly at her for several seconds. 'I invited you here to discuss my involvement with the *Sea Shepherd*. I am not going to talk about ancient history. This is what I am now. It may not be the story you want, but' – he poked his chest with his finger – 'the truth is me now.'

Melissa was taken aback by his attitude. After all, she had picked up her information in press cuttings about him, none of this was new material. She couldn't help wondering why he seemed to be so agitated by what she had said.

'But it's fascinating. This gives the profile some texture. It makes you more interesting. An enigma. It was obviously important to your development.' She drew her finger horizontally down the page in her notebook. 'Here, for example. You went back to Poland again in 1972, after you left college.'

Avery walked across to the door. Charlie had by

70

now appraised things; the situation was deteriorating swiftly. He came from behind the desk and stood beside Melissa. Avery laid his hand on the handle and gripped it.

'The interview is concluded,' he announced brusquely. He opened the door. 'Anything you don't know, make up. Reporters usually do.' With that he turned and walked out.

*   *   *   *   *

The car see-sawed over the cattle grid. Melissa re-adjusted the rearview mirror and caught a final glimpse of the retreating house. She experienced the exhilar-ation of a small triumph. She felt she had come out of the altercation with an advantage over Avery. She acknowledged that her sceptical view was wholly vindicated.

Charlie, on the other hand, was both bewildered and regretful. He seemed to have missed the vital part of the drama that had triggered the escalation to hostility. He had enjoyed Avery's company and thought Avery had liked him in return. It was an odd outcome.

They returned along the same winding country lane that had brought them to the mansion. Charlie rifled Melissa's cassette storage box for something decent to entertain him on the journey back to Bristol. He shuffled the plastic cassette cases in his hand, tutting his disapproval of her musical tastes. Suddenly, Melissa braked and swerved across the road and mounted the verge of a ditch. Charlie looked in front of them.

A TV detector van was approaching in the opposite direction and there wasn't enough room for both

71

vehicles to pass. The van slowed and the driver almost pedalled alongside Melissa's car. She looked at the two men in the front seat.

'They're going to Avery's,' she exclaimed. 'Now can you beat that! Rich as Croesus and hasn't paid his TV licence.'

But Charlie experienced a sudden dread that made him shiver. The cassette boxes slipped from between his fingers.

'That man,' Charlie stammered. 'I know him from somewhere.'

'Which one?' asked Melissa. 'I wouldn't mind meeting either of them.'

'The driver,' Charlie turned and watched through the rear window as the TV van picked up speed and returned to the middle of the road. His mind raced. His teeth bit into his lip as he searched his memory.

'He was at the docks yesterday. I saw him standing there when they took the diver's body away,' Charlie breathed excitedly.

Melissa checked the road behind her and moved off again. She stretched out her hand and picked up a Dire Straits cassette from the pile Charlie was re-ordering. She thrust it into the tape recorder.

'It was a TV van, Charlie. Not an ambulance. Maybe they bear some resemblance to each other,' she suggested soothingly.

'He looks the same because he is the same. I know he is,' Charlie protested. 'And what's more we saw a TV detector van down there, too. We couldn't have made a mistake about that.'

Melissa turned it over in her mind. She tried to resist the compelling temptation to rush headlong at conclusions but already she was taking the strands of events that had taken place and weaving them together. She took the speed down to a steady 40 mph and reviewed her ingredients.

There was Avery, first of all. For no reason at all he flew off the handle when she just mentioned a few facts that everyone knew. Why? He was a banner-waving lefty when he was at college. He was financing a ship that was going to investigate toxic waste levels in the North Sea. The Government, not this one in any case, wouldn't be pinning any medals on his chest for public service. They were one of the worst sinners when it came to polluting the seas. They wouldn't appreciate the publicity. But the ship hadn't even set sail yet, it was still being fitted out down at Avonmouth docks so the authorities need not become jittery for a while yet.

The diver, well . . . THE DIVER! THE DOCKS! THE SEA SHEPHERD!

'You clown!' Melissa yelled, laughing giddily.

Charlie flushed, wounded. 'Who? . . . Me?' he asked.

'You genius!' she shrieked. 'You absolute genius, Charlie. I'm the clown . . . Oh, my, what a bozo I've been! You were right, Charlie. A real bozo.'

She turned down the music and drove in silence for a few minutes. She wanted nothing more than to relish her own brilliant luck, the blissful sensation of her victory over the traps and deceptions that had been set in place to thwart her. She rejoiced in her audacity, her determination, the unfailing inner conviction that had carried her to the heart of a story with awesome reverberations.

She could already see the hordes of reporters pushing

and shoving one another in the first-class Pullman carriages as they sped to Bristol from Fleet Street, the hired coaches with blinded windows conveying an army of press photographers, the screeching helicopter bearing a team of veteran correspondents from whom politicians and spokesmen would flee as, one by one, the cobwebs of deceit were blown away with each penetrating article.

'Try this on for size, Charlie,' Melissa at last began.

She couldn't yet fill in every detail. But the overall shape of the picture was now inescapable. The British intelligence service had Avery and the *Sea Shepherd* under surveillance. They followed Avery and probably intercepted his conversations with the TV vans. The authorities were suspicious of him. Obviously, this was because of his left-wing past which maybe wasn't so dead as Avery wanted us to believe. As part of their intelligence operation they had sent the diver down to investigate the *Sea Shepherd*. The diver had died, perhaps he had been killed. If he was killed, she said, the inescapable conclusion was that Avery had accomplices. These were probably East European agents. What's more, it was now apparent that the *Sea Shepherd* was not exactly what it pretended to be if protecting its secret was worth killing for. So what did Avery have that was so important to the East? If Avery's company had designed security systems to protect data then he held the passkeys to vast sources of commercial and military secrets. You didn't have to look any further.

The environmental project was just a smoke screen; the *Sea Shepherd* was a decoy. Its real purpose was to transport Avery's records out of the country. When

74

the *Sea Shepherd* sailed, Avery was going with her. He was going to defect.

'When does she sail, Charlie?' Melissa asked. 'How long have we got?'

SEVEN

Francis Nicholson had set out early, allowing himself time to meander before his appointment. He enjoyed walking. A leisurely stroll in the zoo would compensate in part for the holiday he had been obliged to interrupt.

It was a biting cold late autumn morning. The sky was powder blue and the sun so bright he found himself squinting. He pulled his lambswool scarf above the collar of his loden overcoat to protect his cheeks from chill burn. His mind dwelled on the meeting to come and he tried to define what his aim should be.

He had listened several times to the recording of Avery's conversation with Nestor Greffen. There was something about it that did not gel. He admitted that Avery, naturally, had been disconcerted by the news of his daughter's premature arrival. It was obviously a shock to him. Equally, Avery must have been apprehensive knowing that Greffen may have been directly involved in the death of the diver. This news must have frightened him. And still Nicholson believed there was something that did not add up. He ordered enlargements of the surveillance photographs and had these time-synchronised with the audio tapes. He could not be totally certain but it was possible that Avery had disconnected the microphone himself. It could never be more than speculation, of course. However, the supposed failure of the batteries was doubtful. The battery pack had been examined and was in perfect order. Equipment was prone to fail, Nicholson reminded himself. But did it always fail at so propitious a moment? If Avery had interfered with the microphone what did that indicate?

Nicholson checked his watch. It was 10.26 a.m. He halted and studied the screeching parakeets in the wiremesh aviary. Their squawking subsided while they observed him. The zoo was a labyrinth of lanes and footpaths. Nicholson looked from side to side for a signpost to the aquarium. He thrust his gloved hands into his pockets and began walking briskly towards the nearest junction.

Their rendezvous was for 10.30. Avery was already in position when Nicholson entered the aquarium building. His leather heels clicked on the stone floor and echoed around the dark room. The fish seemed monstrous, like a collection of mutants, prehistoric, unaesthetic.

'I'll be frank with you, Mr Avery,' Nicholson said loudly. His voice reverberated off the glass. 'I think we may have been too rash,' he continued, adjusting his projection to a more intimate register. 'Circumstances made us put all our eggs in one basket. I must tell you that there are risks involved in this operation.'

Avery was cordial, affable. 'I understand that, Mr Nicholson.'

'And do you understand that Greffen might have

killed our diver,' Nicholson said with slow deliberation, 'and that he may try to kill you also?'

Avery didn't hesitate. 'I think the risk is worth the result.'

Nicholson admired his courage. It was clear that he had already pondered this possibility and reconciled himself to it. But it was Nicholson's obligation to remind him of the dangers.

'And I have to say that I'm not convinced it is worth that result.'

'I mean the result for me,' returned Avery. 'My daughter. All this,' he said, extending his hands to indicate the entire charade in which he had become a participant, 'is just a means to an end. One way or another, there had to be a ransom to pay.'

'Then you'll go on?' asked Nicholson.

'Yes.'

'I'm grateful. Thank you,' Nicholson responded warmly. He admired Avery's nobility.

Avery closed the bottom button on his overcoat. 'Is that what you wanted to tell me?' he asked, preparing to return to the cold.

Nicholson touched Avery's arm with his gloved hand. 'In part, yes . . . I felt I had to be open with you because some new development seems imminent. GCHQ at Cheltenham have advised us of a sudden flurry of messages. We don't know exactly what the contents are at this moment, but the traffic indicates intensified activity.'

Nicholson peeled off his glove and his hand felt around inside his coat. He withdrew his wallet. He opened the soft calf leather and handed Avery a white business card.

'Remember. It is never too late to call everything off. If you call this number the operation will be suspended immediately and we shall rescue you.'

Avery stretched out his hand to take the card but changed his mind. He declined it.

'I shan't be needing it,' he replied.

'Perhaps not,' the other man agreed. 'But I require you to have it,' he told Avery as he inserted the card into the breast pocket of Avery's coat.

*   *   *   *   *

Greffen looked up at the blind photo-electric projector and winked at it. The glass doors slid sideways on their invisible runners and he pushed his shopping trolley down the ramp. His hands gripped the metal bar tightly as a jammed wheel made the trolley lurch to the right.

It would be his last excursion to the hypermarket and he had taken the opportunity to provide himself with some of the groceries he would most miss when he returned to his own country. He had bought five pounds of Lapsang tea, a dozen jars of coarse-cut marmalade, forty-eight rolls of soft toilet tissue and, his favourite indulgence, three dozen boxes of Bournville chocolate fingers.

He had not been home for over twenty years. His homesickness had waned after the first three years. He had never married and his only surviving relative had been his mother. She had died of tuberculosis fourteen years ago. With her death his yearning to return had left him for good. There was no home waiting for him, no wife and no children. He would have to try to find a small one-bedroom flat. It would be in the centre of the city, on one of the busiest streets. The one circumstance that had blighted his residence in England had been the restrictions his bosses had placed on his choice of neighbourhood. He lived in a bungalow on a new housing estate in the suburbs and hated it.

He wondered what he would miss about England. He acknowledged that it certainly had the best television of any place he had visited in the world. He would miss that. He liked the documentaries and the news programmes. He was fond, also, of the comedy programmes and his tastes had evolved over time. Of course, he loved – didn't everyone? – the double acts, 'The Two Ronnies' and 'Morecambe and Wise'. They were simply variations on the incomparable Laurel and Hardy. Slapstick comedy disregarded national frontiers and cultural boundaries. Everyone had at one time a special friend. Laurel and Hardy were the prototypes of all friendships: affection and exasperation.

Greffen pushed his trolley over the black tarmac following the white lines laid out for parking spaces. He had to kick it from time to time to prevent the cart veering off into the rain gutter. He spotted Avery's Jaguar and altered his course.

'You're breaking our agreement,' Avery blustered as he lowered the electrically powered windows. 'We could be spotted easily out here, it's too exposed.'

Greffen haughtily raised his eyebrows. He walked around the front of the car and opened the passenger door. He almost had to lie down to squeeze inside. He pulled the door closed.

'This isn't an everyday business situation, Richard,'

he reminded Avery needlessly. 'We are dealing in espionage, not selling washing machines. I telephoned you because we must talk.' He shifted awkwardly in the deep seat pulling his belt buckle from under his thigh.

'What's so urgent?' Avery questioned. 'The *Sea Shepherd* isn't sailing for at least another month. It could have waited until this evening.'

Greffen gave him a pained smile. 'We are bringing things forward to a more convenient time.'

Avery was adamant. 'The repairs take time. I can't bring forward delivery agreements. We'll just have to sit it out.'

'We won't need the *Sea Shepherd* any more,' Greffen announced categorically. He rummaged in his raincoat pocket and brought out a packet of cigarettes and an envelope. He pressed down the car cigarette-lighter and then handed the envelope to Avery. 'I have something for you.'

Avery opened it slowly and took out a Polaroid snapshot of his daughter, Magda. She looked grim and exhausted, there was a tide mark of dirt around her neck. She held in front of her a newspaper. It was this morning's edition of *Today*. Avery winced. His mouth dried.

'If you'll let me have that back,' said Greffen. He reached and retrieved the photograph. He lit his cigarette with the lighter and then rolled the photograph into a small tube and planted it on top of the red, smouldering heating element inside the lighter. The picture began to crack and deform. Greffen tossed it out of the window into the gutter when it was alight.

'You see?' he declared. 'We have fulfilled our offer. The girl is here in England waiting for you. Why prolong her misery and yours?'

Avery was shattered, speechless. He looked at the shoppers calmly, mechanically, going about their simple uncomplicated lives.

'I have some new instructions. In addition to the design for the new Centaur programme, we would also like the complete list of all your company's clients with the full plans of their system modifications.'

Avery's mind swelled with panic. He felt numbness all over his body as if he had plunged into a pool of ice-cold water.

'It's just completely out of the question. I cannot do it. You're asking me to give you the doorkey to every civilian and government database in the country, the records of every citizen, defence strategies, more.'

Greffen tried to ease the situation with humour. 'We're a nation of bureaucrats, after all, Richard. Our people thrive on files. They have an insatiable appetite for paperwork.'

Avery shook his head, weary. 'It's impossible. You know it is.'

'Nothing's impossible,' Greffen countered cheerily. 'Not in this world.' He raised the handle on the door and half-opened it. 'I think you will help, Richard. When you think it over.'

Greffen stood in front of his shopping cart and looked around at the gigantic food store with articulated refrigerator lorries lining up to deliver their goods at the rear in readiness for the weekend crush. It reminded him of the prize that was about to drop into his hands. Millions of items, enough to provide sustenance to his organisation for years to come. And he looked at his basket, the small mountain of delicacies he would savour in the months to come.

'When?' cried Avery. 'When, Nestor . . . ?'

'This afternoon. Come for tea. I've got something just right for afternoon tea.'

* * * * *

An involuntary smile broke across Galbraith's face. 'I want two cars with Avery all day,' he shouted, 'starting now. NOW!'

The watchers dropped their newspapers on the sofas where they sat. The secretaries grabbed their telephones and began dialling numbers. Hughes ran across the room and placed himself in front of the radio microphone. The entire office was galvanised by the commotion as if they had just heard a typhoon was about to hit them.

'What do you reckon, Mr Galbraith,' queried Hughes. 'Is Avery going to deliver?'

Galbraith, a meteor of nerves, excitement and adrenalin, sprinted across the room. He stood in front of Hughes. The muscles in his calves twitched.

'How should I know?' he barked tersely. 'I'm not a damned mind reader.'

Galbraith stormed out of the room to give Nicholson the news of the latest unsuspected bombshell.

Hughes waited until Galbraith had slammed the door. He barked in the direction of the two watchers preparing themselves for another daytime shift in the cold. 'And he's no magician, either. He'd better get to that girl and bring her to Avery before Avery gives

Greffen an early Christmas present. Or his goose is cooked.'

Galbraith bucked the stairs to the upper floor two at a time. He had worked it out for himself a long time since. He knew there had been no battery failure. Avery had simply jettisoned his microphone the minute Greffen had mentioned his daughter two days ago. His reason was transparent. Avery had known from that moment that he would co-operate with Greffen. The man had no principles.

Galbraith had taken the precaution of attaching a listening device to Avery's car. His suspicion and contempt were well-founded. He allowed himself another smirk of private satisfaction. He was righteously vindicated. He peered down at Nicholson's bald pate. The old man had received the latest information with a resigned silence. He gazed up into Galbraith's red angular face.

'It's my view, Martin,' he said with unexpected sociability, 'but I consider it quite possible Avery will do as Greffen asks.'

Galbraith breathed in deeply to staunch any expression of his hostility toward Nicholson. He was frankly incredulous, but contented himself with a mild endorsement.

'They're not trustworthy, that type,' he agreed. 'Once a radical, always a radical.'

Nicholson shook his head. He stated with mild reproof, 'You're mistaken, Martin.'

'How?' Galbraith asked spikily.

'Because you ignore the human dimension.' Nicholson motioned to Galbraith to take a seat. He paused for a moment, assessing Galbraith.

'You are a fine intelligence officer,' he said warmly. 'You were shrewd to bug his car. I should have thought of that. But you lack an understanding of the human heart; you diminish your effectiveness by withholding your sympathy. The hunter must be able to put himself in the place of the hunted. You should be able to anticipate his next move but you should also understand his motives.'

Galbraith listened unmoved, cold. Only results mattered. Let the psychiatrists sort out the criminals' emotional problems. Galbraith had no room for emotionally disturbed traitors.

Nicholson raised his voice. 'Avery has a new loyalty, his daughter. And a new master . . . his own guilt at having deserted her. He is no longer the same man as when we started running this operation. Then he was just a man who had everything. Now he is a father who can offer everything. This is fundamental.'

Galbraith shrugged his shoulders dismissively. 'He's still betraying his country's secrets,' he retorted. 'Might as well hang for a sheep as a lamb.'

Nicholson was silent. He knew that Galbraith was impervious to his attempts to persuade him. This sort of man only understood the rigid imposition of authority. He had no room for questions. To Galbraith, the world was black and white; he could be accommodated easily on either side. Nicholson had failed to convince Galbraith with his argument: the only worthwhile distinction between the two opposing protagonists was, precisely, humanity. This was what, ultimately, Galbraith was recruited to defend. It was the nub of the rift between East and West.

'What do we do now?' Galbraith wanted to know. 'Hope he'll turn himself in?'

Nicholson met his scornful gaze. 'You find the daughter before he does.'

EIGHT

'Once I get in,' explained Charlie, 'the next problem will be making it think that I'm Avery.'

Daniel and Melissa looked on expectantly as Charlie punched Richard Avery's telephone number into his modem. He pressed the switch and the modem began dialling.

Melissa experienced an uncomfortable *déjà vu*. We have been here before, she reminded herself. She recalled the attempt to raid the National Police Computer just a couple of days ago in her office. Her expectations for success this time were not high. But this was their only hope.

The loudspeaker attached to the computer suddenly stirred into life. They could hear the amplified ringing tone as the connection was made to Avery's domestic micro. It rang six times and then there followed a loud whining noise.

The cursor flashed several times and then raced across the screen revealing a message:

ENTER PASSWORD NOW, PLEASE

Melissa was now well versed in most of the illegal aspects of computer hacking and knew this was the only hurdle that lay before them. She had come prepared, and in the crook of her arm held an edition of *Who's Who* with a slip of paper between the pages where Richard Avery's entry appeared.

'Okay,' Charlie whooped, 'let's tell it I'm Avery and see if it shakes my hand or bites it.' He typed in the name RICHARD. The message disappeared and reappeared.

'Tough,' sympathised Daniel. 'Good try, though,' he added. 'Imaginative.'

Charlie snarled at him and tried a second possibility: SEA SHEPHERD. He met the same reaction from the computer. Unfriendliness.

Melissa opened her massive volume and ran her finger across the page. 'Try this,' she said. 'His mother's name was Jean. Jean Howard.'

Who's Who was one of the hacker's most valuable tools. Daniel was close to the mark even though he didn't realise it. People were extremely careless when it came to selecting their passwords to access secure databases. Either they used daft phrases like 'I love me' or 'Kiss Kiss' or else they fell back on personal information which they foolishly thought they alone knew. A popular favourite was their mother's maiden name or their own confirmation name. These latter were not likely to be guessed at in the normal haphazard course of opportunist hacking when someone was just joyriding through databases. But when the target was specific, hackers had numerous means of discovering the information they needed. They would even make hoax telephone calls claiming to be credit agencies checking on a credit reference. Sometimes they would pretend to be competition organisers and ask for a maiden name in order to verify a prizewinner.

Charlie turned to Melissa. 'Let's hope it gives us a couple more goes before it kicks us out.' He typed in JEAN. This met with the same response. 'Nope,' he said, regretfully.

'It's not a fruit machine, you know,' Daniel chimed in pessimistically. 'You can't keep trying until you get a winner. It'll chuck you out soon.'

Charlie knew this only too well. Most computers were programmed to accept three attempts at a password and then they automatically disconnected the line. Fortunately, their target was Avery's own home micro which didn't have the capacity to terminate the connection once it was made and then dial back to the telephone number that corresponded to the password. Many computer operators were woken at four in the morning by their database returning a call they had never placed. Not only were they jolted from their sleep but simultaneously they learned their systems had been invaded. It was like being pickpocketed in your own lounge.

Charlie knew they must ration their guesses. Melissa began to despair as she saw her only chance of ensnaring Avery slowly fade away. Charlie racked his brains; Melissa bit her nails.

Daniel was becoming restless. He scratched his ear and unhooked the sheaves of data about Charlie's fish. Charlie heard the rustle of the paper and snapped sharply, 'I'm trying to concentrate here.' Daniel threw him a wounded stare. And then it zoomed into Charlie's memory. Without saying a word he started typing.

J . . A . . C . . K   D . . E . . M . . P . . S . . E . . Y

Charlie mumbled to himself, 'The first fish I ever bought'.

Melissa gave vent to her frustration. 'What are you rabbiting on about, Charlie.'

But her eye was drawn to the little rectangular cursor on the screen which throbbed and vanished. It reappeared like a comet in the sky trailing a tail in its wake.

HELLO BOSS

PRESS ANY KEY TO CONTINUE

Charlie snapped his fingers in the air. 'We're in! We're in! What do we do now?' he shouted triumphantly.

Melissa muzzed his hair affectionately. 'Can you ask it when Avery made his last entry?'

Charlie pressed a key and a diary page appeared on screen. In a little box in the top left-hand corner the screen showed the actual time and the time when the last access took place. 'Easy as pie,' said Charlie nonchalantly. 'Anything else?'

The three of them scrutinised the runic entries, abbreviations for business meetings, product codes, reminders of telephone calls to be made, etc. It was puzzling to know what use to make of the information they had now successfully unlocked. Melissa drew her breath and pointed her finger at one of the entries on the screen: ELITE'S P.M.

'Elite Bakery? The man is going to defect with a bag of secrets and a sponge cake,' she proclaimed in disbelief.

Charlie pointed to the screen record of the last entry. 'Shall we ask what he did at 10.23 a.m. this morning?'

Daniel cleared his throat in exasperation. 'Do we clean our teeth with a toothbrush?' he growled impatiently.

'Print me a copy,' commanded Melissa.

'And don't spare the horses!' Daniel added drily.

The printer whirred into action, spitting out the paper roll like a mad bus conductor. Melissa reached across to a bookshelf and located the Bristol and Avon telephone directory. As she flicked through the book searching for the number of the confectioner's, Charlie called to her.

'Listen, Melissa . . . Avery requested a complete listing of all his company's clients *and* copies of the maintenance handbooks for each system.'

Melissa revolved on her heels and clapped her hands together, staggered.

'We were right. Bang on the nail. The guy's a spy for sure. He's giving them everything but the lightbulbs!' she exclaimed. Her excitement was cut short when she recalled the most recent conundrum. She gasped. 'But what's the bakery got to do with all this?'

Charlie gazed blankly at her. He could absorb no more. He had squeezed the last drop of ingenuity and invention from his reeling brain.

Daniel considered the pair of them, astounded how easily their common sense had deserted them, left them stranded, gawping.

'Why don't we go and ask?' he piped up breezily.

*　　*　　*　　*　　*

Brrr . . . Brrr   Brrr . . . Brrr   Brrr . . . Brrr

Avery heard a door shut downstairs. Rachel was on her way to answer the telephone. She could not bring herself to tell even a white lie. She would say he was at home. He would have to answer the call himself.

He lifted the receiver. He didn't bother saying 'Hello'. He knew who it would be. He held the telephone away from his ear and heard Galbraith raucously calling his name.

'Richard . . . are you there?'

Avery depressed the button to terminate the call. He laid the earpiece on the desk. It made a buzzing noise for a few seconds. Then there were clicking sounds. The line was being monitored. The phone was bugged.

He raised the lid of his satin-polished aluminium suitcase. The metal shell was filled with one giant continuous length of computer stationery like an enormous concertina. Avery placed a few pairs of socks around the edges to stop the heavy package shifting from side to side. Next he clicked home the tumblers and spun the combination wheels.

He wasn't angry on discovering his telephone was bugged. He wasn't even dismayed. He had sensed Galbraith's hostility towards him. It had begun as soon as they first met. Galbraith viewed any civilian who came into his orbit as tainted. Avery knew the man disliked and resented him. Probably his suspicions had been groundless when the operation first started. They were proved right now. Perhaps Galbraith, Avery speculated, had allowed himself a moment's self-congratulation.

He was embarked now on a compact he would follow

through to its conclusion. Avery knew that Galbraith would try his utmost to prevent the exchange taking place. Avery had already reflected on what course he would follow if the deal were to be sabotaged by Galbraith's intervention. He would seek Greffen's protection, and defect.

Only his daughter mattered to him now. Greffen's guignolesque photograph of Magda had the effect, paradoxically, of making her fully alive to Avery for the first time. Until then she existed only in the hinterlands of Avery's active emotions. The newspaper in the foreground had been a melodramatic touch. Greffen had probably selected the newspaper only because it was brightly coloured and easily identifiable. But it might just as well have been a note written in felt pen hanging around her neck. Magda was a hostage. Avery's computer files were the ransom.

If he had not made the decision at the beginning to inform the police after Greffen's first contact, things would be very different. Avery might have been able to arrange some clandestine transfer of the information Greffen requested. But he knew he would not have been capable of such treachery. There was no fortune which could have tempted him. Ironically, it was Greffen and not Galbraith who had understood this. Therefore Greffen bargained with the girl, cleaving his loyalties, confident that Avery would splinter along the fault line of his weakness; his heart.

Galbraith had both complicated and purified matters but, having precipitated Avery to make a stark choice, Galbraith's presence unexpectedly brought with it a new clarity. It was no longer a simple question of exchanging a ransom for a hostage. Avery realised that by rejecting Magda as his child fifteen years ago he had also stolen her childhood, a part of her life. His selfishness had made her a half-being, a zombie. Now it was within his power to resurrect her and restore her to life by breathing into her the love of a father. To give her life he would sacrifice his own. He would return to her home. By liberating his heart he could endure the enslavement of his freedom.

He had made no preparations to take anything with him. He would leave the house with no more than he usually took to his office. The aluminium case sat on a chair. He went to his closet and took a cashmere jacket from a hanger. It would be his only indulgence.

He grasped the handle of the suitcase and carried it downstairs and placed it in the boot of his Jaguar. He wouldn't be using this again either. He slammed the lid.

Rachel appeared on the terrace; she was rapt in her thoughts. He smiled at her and his heart shuddered. She had been the ballast of his life.

'I was thinking of a baked alaska,' she remarked absently.

She quickly cast her eye over the brand new car. 'If I treated my oven the way you treat that car of yours . . .' she reprimanded him lightly.

'I'm on edge,' he apologised. 'There's a tough day ahead. I didn't mean to make a racket.'

Rachel cleaned her hands, brushing them against the sides of her apron. She looked at her palms and turned them over to inspect her nails.

'I think I'll bake,' she declared. 'It's very therapeutic.' She gave him a wave with her head and returned to the kitchen.

Avery inserted the car key into the boot lock and turned it. He walked around to the side of the car and got in behind the steering wheel. After turning on the ignition he edged forward a few metres and stopped in front of the kitchen. They had outlawed saying goodbye to one another; it seemed gratuitous. He tapped twice lightly on the horn. Beep. Beep.

Rachel watched him accelerate away down the long path and over the cattle grid.

*   *   *   *   *

Daniel flared his nostrils. he drew into his throat the sweet strong aroma of yeast, cloves, caramel and cinnamon. The air was speckled with fine flour dust. He looked at the sloping wooden trays filled with crusty cobs like spinsters' bonnets and golden tin loaves with regularly spaced ridges which the baker had slashed with his knife. A buxom woman in a white overall and wearing a white hairnet buffeted the swing door with her hips and placed herself behind the counter. She gently laid down a broad white cake box with *Elite Bakers* printed across the lid in gilt-edged scalloped lettering.

'Here we are, dear,' she said. 'Now you be sure to tell Mr Avery there's a dozen free range eggs in there. And I can guarantee you every raisin comes from a good democratic country.'

Daniel slid the box carefully off the counter and brought it to rest on his forearm while his other hand clasped the box around two of its corners. 'I'll give him the message, don't worry,' he told her confidently.

He sucked in air as he took its weight and steadied himself for a second like a weightlifter before he snatches the barbell. Daniel wanted her to be reassured

97

that he would take painstaking care with the precious object. 'Thank you,' he added politely, a model gentleman. The lady came round from behind her counter and opened the door for him.

Daniel carried the cake to the car and passed it through the front window to Charlie. He settled down on the back seat and pulled the door to.

'Let's get a move on,' he said eagerly. 'She'll work out she's been conned in a minute.'

Melissa took off at a sedate pace to deflect any suspicions. Once she had turned the corner she said. 'Off with the lid and see what's in there.'

Charlie obeyed. He felt he was pillaging someone's bedroom. He felt like a burglar. He was plunging his hands into secrets he had no right to probe. He was a confidence trickster. But he was also desperately curious; as he lifted the lid he prayed he would find an innocent cake.

'I can't take my eyes off the road, we'll all be killed. What is it?'

Charlie sat with the box in his lap and the lid held aloft between his fingers. He stared at the pink-iced cake with a red ribbon tied in a bow around the buttercup-coloured marzipan.

'It's a cake,' he stated, relieved.

'It can't be!' Melissa protested. 'It can't be,' she repeated, incredulous.

Daniel leaned forward and poked his head between the valley dividing the two front seats. 'Maybe it's a bomb?' he suggested flippantly.

Melissa was crestfallen. She could not imagine anything in which Avery was involved being other than some intricate deceit. Somehow, she was convinced,

98

the cake – real or false – was the centrepiece of some gigantic ploy of Avery's. She was not going to be a victim of one of his clever ruses.

Charlie tried to comfort her. 'Maybe it's filled with microdots?' he ventured.

Daniel tutted, rebuking their fabulous inventions. 'Why don't we ask his daughter?' he asked plainly.

'Because he doesn't have one. He was never married.' Melissa was finding their ridiculous promptings exasperating.

Melissa didn't intimidate Daniel in the slightest. She wasn't his aunt; he wasn't going to be cowed by her tongue-lashing just because she leapt to all the wrong conclusions.

'No?' he said stiffly. Daniel prodded her in the shoulder, knowing she could not retaliate while she was still driving. 'So who's Magda, then?' he trumpeted.

Melissa steered the car off the road and parked on the kerb. She jerked up the handbrake and ripped the lid off the cake-box. The corners of her mouth tightened. She stared at the cake.

Slivers of emerald-coloured icing decorated the surface of the fruit cake like a matchstick doodle. The message spelled: WELCOME HOME MAGDA, FATHER.

An image popped up on a screen in Melissa's mind. She remembered going into Avery's bedroom to return the telephone message from her bleeper. She saw herself examining the crystal glass phials of expensive men's perfumes on his dresser. She reached out and, with the telephone clamped between her ear and her shoulder, she picked up a silver photoframe decorated with art-deco angels and looked at a picture of a scrawny blonde-haired teenage girl. She'd hardly noticed the photograph; she'd been looking for the hallmark on the reverse side of the frame.

'The girl in the picture!' she exploded. 'The return of the prodigal daughter!' she cried.

She turned and faced Daniel. He looked her back in the face. Her eyes seemed glazed. He thought she was going to slap his face. But she didn't. She kissed him on the forehead.

'Daniel. You just made my day.'

NINE

Melissa rolled her eyes. 'It's half term. I'm lumbered with the baby sitting,' she explained apologetically.

Mr Greene, the docks' press officer, sniffed at Charlie and Daniel who followed a few yards behind them on the quayside. Daniel scootered along with one foot on his skateboard. Mr Greene cast him a disapproving look.

Mr Greene was a small, pneumatic man with a round face; he had bags of fat on his cheeks that made him look like a frog. He wore a hand-knitted, V-neck pullover that stretched across his round chest teasing at the stitches. The pattern on his shirt beneath was visible. He continued with his recitation.

'The port processes over a million tonnes of petroleum in any given year. Timber imports account for almost twenty per cent of the total trade volume. We handle about a quarter of a million tonnes of imported ore and coal per year. Are you getting all this down?' he addressed Melissa, surprised at her lack of a notebook or mini tape recorder.

'I'm blessed with total recall,' she lied confidently.

Mr Greene snorted sceptically. 'We had a coal ship in from Eastern Europe only this morning, as a matter of fact. They're one of our biggest coal importers these days. I expect you'd be interested to see it?' he asked.

'Fascinated,' replied Melissa, rather too quickly.

'This way, then. If you'd like to follow me.'

They were led along a wharf. Melissa skipped every few yards to keep abreast with Mr Greene. She sifted among the debris and miscellaneous tidbits in her mind trying to find subjects to fill the gaps in conversation.

'I expect lots of ships come in from the Atlantic ports,' she commented.

'Oh, indeed,' answered Mr Greene. 'And geography was particularly kind to us in former times.' He continued volubly with a potted history of the port and Bristol's maritime traditions. At last, he pointed to the coal ship he wanted to show them.

Its mooring was only one pier distant from the berth of the *Sea Shepherd*. Melissa's eyes flicked to and fro between the two ships.

Melissa flattered Mr Greene and, impressed by her obvious natural sympathy for nautical history, he left the three of them to take a leisurely walk around the port. 'I'll keep them on a tight leash,' she said to him reassuringly, indicating the two boys.

'We're only *assuming* she's on board the ship,' Daniel said doubtfully.

Melissa scotched his defeatism immediately. 'Oh, she's there, Daniel, all right. She's the missing piece of the puzzle.'

Charlie held his hands over his eyes in a peak and tried to detect any trace of human activity on the deck. 'Maybe Daniel's right. We could have made a mistake.'

Melissa, this time, knew she could not be wrong, knew she was never really wrong at all. She had invested too much of her own integrity to be so utterly contradicted at this stage.

'No, no,' she insisted. 'Don't you see? Avery almost told us as much himself. When I asked him about those trips to Eastern Europe when he was a student, what did he say?'

Charlie did not remember.

'He called it a youthful romance,' she reminded him, quoting Avery. 'He's not giving this information away because he's political. But I suppose he must have fallen in love when he was there and now they've found the child . . . and that's how they're blackmailing him.'

She interrupted herself. A pure and simple explanation entered her mind. It absolved Avery and she had to wrestle with her own temperament to admit it.

'He's done this to regain a daughter, not to betray his country. But that's the price they're asking,' she said with a tremor in her voice. 'He even confessed as much to us.'

Charlie screwed up his eyes and confirmed what he first thought was just a mirage, a wilful projection. 'I take everything back. She's there!'

In the distance a young girl was leaning against the rail on the deck of the coal ship. A broad woman with her hair pulled tightly back and fastened with a clasp was standing beside her, looming over her like a predator.

Melissa shepherded the two boys around a corner and out of sight from the ship. She rapidly sketched out a plan for the two boys. Daniel took off on his skateboard back along the road they had just followed.

Melissa made Charlie take off his Benetton sweatshirt.

Putting her arm around Charlie's shoulder, Melissa relaxed her body and shifted her weight onto Charlie. They returned along the same road and continued to slowly walk past the coal ship. Melissa swung her other arm and rubbed the small of her back and winced. Charlie's sweatshirt was lashed around her waist and formed a basket which held her jacket. To anyone who glanced at her casually Melissa was in a quite advanced condition of pregnancy.

The girl saw the young woman hobbling with careful steps, and gave her a friendly wave. Charlie pricked his ears and heard the distant whining drone of a police siren. The girl, too, heard the wailing siren. She turned from side to side, looking. Then her mouth opened and she screamed in German. She clawed at her guardian's sleeve and shouted incomprehensibly. The woman turned her head and saw a boy on a skateboard propelling himself with all his might.

She saw a pregnant young woman who was walking directly into the path of the speeding skater. She too shouted out. The pair of them rushed forward towards the gangway that led down to the quay.

The boy swerved around the corner of the warehouse and slammed into the pregnant woman who reeled and tumbled to the ground with a penetrating shriek. The guardian ran down the gangway steps and dashed across the road.

Melissa lay spreadeagled on the ground, moaning. The two boys looked at one another with mortified expressions. The woman knelt down on the ground and held Melissa's head in her hand. The young girl stood on the top steps of the gangway with a distraught look creasing her features. She watched as her guardian straightened Melissa's crumpled legs and bent over her stomach.

The two boys started to shout. 'Come on, Run! *Run!*'

The girl on the steps looked bewildered. She watched her guardian raise her head, stunned also. The two boys were screaming hoarsely like gamblers with their train fare on a failing horse. The woman began to ease herself off her knees and the girl saw the pregnant woman raise herself and grab her guardian by the lapels of her coat. The woman tipped headlong onto the ground.

Charlie screamed, 'MAGDA! . . . MAGDA!'

Melissa struggled with the woman, scissoring her around the waist with both arms. She called out to the girl. 'Run! . . . Run! . . . Magda, *please.*'

Suddenly the girl realised the accident was all a fake. She hesitated for a second, then raced down the gangway and away from the ship and her captors.

Her guardian tore herself free from Melissa's weak embrace. She bawled out in Polish, summoning the crew of the ship. Daniel remounted his skateboard and launched himself at her like a ball at a skittle. She toppled a second time to the ground.

Everyone turned as they heard the screeching of car tyres. Galbraith propelled himself out of the door of his car and hurtled towards the group, not knowing which one to arrest first.

*　　*　　*　　*　　*

The sun glinted off the metal suitcase, the fierce reflection spinning a dazzling light. Avery checked his watch. It was close on three in the afternoon. He had driven around for two hours in the straggling country lanes. He had taken a detour to avoid the easy detection of his brash car in the city centre, so had not been able to collect the cake he ordered. Anyway, the rich taste improved with time. Avery gripped the door handle and turned the knob clockwise and entered Greffen's office.

The figure who faced him across the room, sitting on a filing cabinet jolted him. It was the tiresome reporter with the ambitious ideas. Suddenly he knew everything had been spoiled. He was only surprised that his avenging angel should turn out to be her – and that the boy was with her.

'I can't explain . . . You won't understand.' He spoke with resignation. 'I don't suppose you want to anyhow. You have your big story now.'

Melissa slid off the metal cabinet and walked across to him. She closed her eyes and drew herself up straight. She wanted to talk with him, to sit for hours with him and listen to him weave for her alone the baroque tapestry of his hidden life. She said simply, 'I understand . . . I understand now.' Her mouth parted in a quick smile. '*Do* I have a surprise for you.'

Charlie looked at him. Avery was puzzled above all by the boy's presence. He hadn't thought Charlie was the type who would want to witness his humiliation. Charlie gestured with his head towards the stairs. Avery climbed them, walking like a sleepwalker.

Upstairs, Greffen was sitting in a wooden swivel chair. He looked impassive but dignified. His expression did not change when he saw Avery. Galbraith was barking into the telephone with animation.

'I don't have any worries about being unorthodox,'

he was saying. 'You can call it insubordination if you like, yes . . .'

Tony Hughes touched Avery on the sleeve. 'Shall I take that, Mr Avery? I don't think you'll be needing it now.' Avery yielded the suitcase.

Galbraith swung around with the phone still in his hand and saw Avery. He looked at him with undisguised rancour. 'Avery's just walked in . . .' he announced into the telephone. He stared hostilely at him. 'Mr Nicholson expresses his thanks and requires me to tell you that this is the end of the matter. However, I require for my own satisfaction to express to you that in my opinion you're a traitor and I'd sooner see you locked up.'

Hughes coughed politely and gestured to Avery to mount the next flight of stairs. 'I'd also like to echo Mr Nicholson's sentiments and express our thanks.' Avery turned and walked to the stairs. He noticed then that Greffen was handcuffed to the chair.

The smell of coffee crept into his nose as he climbed the third set of stairs. Downstairs he could hear Galbraith still pouring his frustration into the telephone. 'I'm delighted you heard me. Delighted.'

Avery stood outside the closed door for a moment. He turned the handle and walked into the room.

Magda was sitting eating biscuits, wearing a policewoman's cap on her head. In her other hand was a fistful of playing cards. She laid one of the cards on the table and looked challengingly into the policewoman's eyes.

'Snap,' she chimed.

She was pleased with herself. She looked proud and happy.

She raised her head and saw Avery.

'Snap! Snap! Snap!' she shouted.

Her father could not hold back his tears. He wept.